I'll Sp<

Brianne,

Take a look into the mind of a
Killer

BDH

B. D. Harris

ISBN-13: 978-0692454473

ISBN-10: 0692454470

Easytime Publishing

Lake Havasu City, Arizona

DEDICATION

This book is dedicated to the exceptional men and woman who serve this country in a law enforcement career, leading by example. Almost all of which are selfless, empathetic, sympathetic, professional and ethical human beings. You rarely receive the recognition you do not expect, but truly deserve.

THANK YOU

I would like to thank,

My wife Angie, for the countless hours you spent editing and correcting, the input you provided to make this book great and for the title.

My children, Brian Jr., Nathan, Maddie, and Lexi for your support and encouragement.

Paul Bailey at EasytimePublishing.com for all your advice and help in putting things together.

The Kalispell Police Department, Lincoln County Sheriff's Office, Spokane County Sheriff's Office, Airway Heights Corrections Center, and Washington Corrections Center for Woman for providing me the training and experiences that made this book possible.

The graphic designer of the cover Andrei Bat at eze.graphics@yahoo.com for a fantastic job on the cover.

Especially to every officer I worked with in my career. I learned from each of you, whether you had one day or 30 years on the job. Be safe.

CHAPTER ONE

"Hello, Hello, Hello," Sue Wilkins said into the phone. "Zoe are you alright?"

The tone of his wife's voice made Dan Wilkins fear that something was terribly wrong.

Zoe, what's going on?" Sue asked. "Please talk to me dear. What's going on?"

The line went dead.

"What's wrong honey?" Dan asked.

"Something is wrong with Zoe," Sue said. "We need to call the police in Seattle. Zoe was struggling with someone and I heard a crash before the phone went dead."

Sometimes one phone call can mess up your whole day. On the day that Zoe Wilkins died, she called her parents.

"Maybe she simply butt dialed," Sue Wilkins said. "All I heard were sounds of a possible struggle. I tried to call back, but there was no answer."

Officer Stan Brooks sat on one corner of his desk and scratched his thick hair. Being the senior officer on the shift, the strangest calls were frequently directed to him.

He continued to listen to the mother's pleas for help but allowed his mind to return to his past. He had grown up poor in the Midwest to a loving mother. His father was an alcoholic salesman gone nine months out of the year, and his mother was a grocery store cashier. She only made enough money to pay the bills. Brooks didn't play sports or do any extra-curricular activities outside of school because of the cost. He began mowing lawns at the age of fourteen to help his mother pay the rent. When his father was home, Brooks protected her from his continual abuse. He learned at an early age that he had to be tough to survive.

"Can you help me officer?" Sue Wilkins asked with fear in her voice. When she heard no reply, she spoke again. "Officer?"

Shaken from his reverie, Brooks gave Mrs. Wilkins the standard police line about how he would do everything in his power to find

1

answers. With the address in hand, Brooks collected his longtime partner Brian Cooper to investigate the scene.

He and Cooper arrived at the two-story apartment and knocked on the door. No one answered. Brooks peered in the window by the front door and discovered a bloody hand.

"I see a body near the kitchen cabinets. I can see a pool of blood on the floor by the body."

"Let's go inside," Cooper said. "I'll call the medical unit."

What neither Brooks nor Cooper understood was that this case would change them both forever.

When Zoe Wilkins awoke earlier that morning, she saw the sun shining in her bedroom window. She jumped out of bed with a jubilant feeling. Her tumultuous relationship with Chad was over and she finally felt free. She smiled while donning her workout clothes and headed out the door for a run.

The beauty of the morning enhanced Zoe's spirits until she returned home and detected something in her apartment seemed amiss. Zoe stepped on the treadmill in the living room and attached the safety cord. She began her cool down walk and hit the speed dial button on her phone. As she waited for her mother to answer, she heard a noise. She began to turn towards the noise before being struck in the head with a vase, knocking her to the ground. Someone grabbed her around the neck and lifted her to her feet. She reached back and grabbed ahold of the attacker with both hands, digging her nails into his sides.

The attacker held a knife to her throat and dragged her to the bedroom. Zoe feared what may happen in the bedroom and began to fight harder. The attacker threw her into the bedroom door violently flinging it open. He tossed her onto the bed, instructing her to put her hands behind her back. She refused and the knife appeared in front of her eyes. She complied with her attacker and her hands were tied behind her.

The attacker lifted her off the bed and guided her to the kitchen. On the way to the kitchen, Zoe again resisted and the attacker slammed her head into a glass picture frame. The terror Zoe felt at this moment paralyzed her. She decided to comply and hoped she would live. He pushed her into the kitchen.

"I don't carry any money," she told him

"I don't want your money," he said as he plunged the knife into her back.

She felt tremendous pain and gasped. Blood drained out of her back making her knees weak. She felt the warm wet blood running down her back, soaking her shirt. The attacker let go of her as she fell to the floor. She felt a painful pop as she freed one hand from the bindings and tried in vain to get to her cell phone on the treadmill. The pool of blood around her grew by the second. She crawled a few inches and became too weak to continue.

As suddenly as the attack began, her life ended. The killer made a vertical cut on her left shoulder blade that connected to a horizontal cut. He conspicuously placed the note in her right hand before fleeing out the sliding glass door. No one realized he was even in her apartment.

***

Cooper and Brooks entered the unlocked apartment. Brooks approached the body and immediately determined the female was deceased, possibly from a stab wound. Cooper searched the apartment for other victims or suspects and found no one. Fragments of a broken bedroom lamp and pieces of a shattered vase were scattered on the carpet. The treadmill safety cord lay in the hall.

"I found an ID," Brooks said.

"Who is she?" Cooper asked.

"Zoe Wilkins."

She was dressed in yoga pants and a sport bra under a form fitting t-shirt. Zoe wore her running shoes and dried sweat stains were on the neckline and back of her shirt. The treadmill display showed that the emergency cord broke from the machine and activated the auto stop. She appeared to have been running on her treadmill when her attacker struck. She lay on her stomach with her left arm stretched above her head as if she tried to pull herself out of the kitchen towards the front door.

Brooks thought the struggle began in the living room, where a water bottle lay on its side on the floor. He saw drag marks on the carpet from that area to the bedroom. In the bedroom, the bed was made, but the comforter had been wrinkled up.

"The suspect threw her on the bed to tie her up I bet," Brooks said.

"I see rope fibers on the bed and a couple drops of blood."

"Intermittent footprints near the drag marks suggest the suspect forced Zoe to walk back to the kitchen," said Brooks. "I assume she walked back after her arms were tied and before she freed her left hand. She has a small abrasion on her neck. The initial stab wound indicates the blood flowed down her back as if she were standing."

"The broken glass in the hallway came from a wall picture still hanging," said Cooper.

"I would guess that she was thrown into the door," said Brooks. "The handle of the bedroom door punched a hole in the wall from being violently thrown open. She probably fought back."

"Someone showered recently, and left blood on several towels," said Cooper.

While waiting for the Crime Scene Processing Team, Brooks spotted a cut in Zoe's back not far from the stab wound. He saw a long vertical and horizontal cut through her t-shirt that formed the letter L.

They discovered a scrap of paper clutched in her right hand that read, "I am here to kill for fun, from now until the end of the month. If I'm not caught by then, I'll move on and kill again."

Brooks and Cooper feared what the future would hold in the next thirty days leading up to the New Year. Those fears would soon be realized.

CHAPTER 2

When the Crime Scene Processing Team (CSPT) arrived and took over the scene Brooks and Cooper returned to the office to begin paperwork. They debated over who should brief the chief and captain. The captain called Brooks into his office and ended the debate. Cooper laughed to himself.

Cooper was a 25-year veteran of the police department. He grew up in a small Montana town with loving and caring parents. He had always been intelligent and active. At the age of five, he became an all-star for the peewee baseball team. In junior high, he began his football career and earned the name Cooper the Knock-Out King. He knocked out the entire backfield of the opponent's running backs, in one game. They were unable to return to the game after being hit by Cooper. Now he was dealing with the most significant case of his career and didn't want to brief the captain.

"I want to try a cell phone trick," Cooper said to Brooks "You call my phone and leave your phone in your shirt pocket so I can listen to the conversation. I'll put mine on mute so you won't hear anything from my end."

"Impressive idea, I'd love to see if this works," Brooks said. He dialed Cooper's phone and placed his phone in his front pocket as he entered the meeting.

Brooks sat in the captain's chair while the captain closed the door. Brooks stood six feet four inches tall and weighed 250 pounds of solid muscle. The captain seemed miniature at five foot six, 140 pounds. Out of fear of conflict with staff, the captain sat in the visitor's chair during the briefing. Brooks' ten years of experience over the captain made him the alpha male in the room.

"We have a homicide," began Brooks. "The perpetrator restrained the victim prior to stabbing her. We found a note in the victim's hand which indicated this murder may be the beginning of a killing spree."

"Is that your gut feeling or did you find any actual proof?" the captain asked.

"The note indicated that the killer would continue his murderous path until the New Year and planned to disappear. We did find bloody towels in the bathroom. The lab is testing them for DNA. From the appearance of the crime scene, the victim put up a fight. She may contain the killers DNA under her fingernails." Brooks continued the briefing, conscious of the phone in his pocket with Cooper on the other end.

After the meeting, Cooper wanted to know what the captain said.

"I didn't hear the conversation because I answered the office phone," he said.

Brooks told Cooper the events of the meeting and that they were in charge of the case. Cooper and Brooks were hoping that the coroner or CSPT would find the evidence they needed to solve this case without further loss of life.

As they were leaving, the crime scene technicians arrived with photos from the scene. Brooks took copies of the photos in his briefcase and received a call from Zoe's parents before going home.

Brooks received more information from Zoe's parents.

"Mr. Wilkins, thank you for returning my call," Brooks said as he answered the phone. "I know this may not be the best time, but any information you can give me may help me to put the man who killed your daughter behind bars."

Wilkins choked up, but managed to speak with a quivering voice. "Zoe grew up in Houston, Texas. In 6TH grade, she took second place in the science fair, but you probably don't want to hear that, right."

"Even the smallest detail may help sir, please continue," Brooks replied.

"Okay. Well, she entered the science fair every year. In her final year of junior high, she won. Her invention helped people with prosthetics. Anyway, she was so excited about winning she decided to enter the nursing field."

"That's fantastic. What else can you tell me about her?" Brooks asked.

"She played volleyball in junior high. She was good, but kept focus on schoolwork. She achieved a 4.0 GPA in high school. But, how does any of this help you find her killer?" Wilkins asked with a sniffle.

"Understanding what kind of person she is allows us to ask the right questions as we pursue her killer. Can you think of anything else we should know about her?"

"Well, she is athletic. In fact, she received several scholarships from prominent universities. She chose Seattle because of the diversity of their medical classes. She worked as a nurse, but wanted to become a doctor of prosthetic research development. That's about all. She was born in January of 1987, this is her third year of nursing school."

"How about recent boyfriends or acquaintances Mr. Wilkins?" Brooks asked.

"She's been dating a boy named Chad but they broke up, I'm sorry I don't know any of her friends,"

"Thank you, Mr. Wilkins, you've been a big help. If you think of anything else, please call me," Brooks completed the call and headed home.

He arrived home to be greeted by his former girlfriend Pam. With her hair still wet from a shower and wearing only one of his t-shirts, she handed him a drink and gave him a kiss. He entered his house. This is not an unusual greeting for Pam. When they dated regularly, he gave her a key and told her to come over anytime. She would often meet him at the door wearing nothing at all. Brooks set down his briefcase and kissed her passionately.

"I wanted to stop by because I am going to be gone for a month," she said.

With Pam's help, Brooks forgot about the case for nearly two hours. Later, in the afterglow of sex, he told Pam about the events of the day. He didn't mention the specific details of the case.

She grew accustomed to hearing the cases Brooks worked and knew not to interrupt. When he finished she told a story about a former client of hers who used to come to the club where she danced.

"For some reason, all the bills he gave the girls were sticky," Pam said smiling. "He would stick the bill to the girl's hand and the money would stay. After months of the guy coming into the club, we found out that he worked with adhesives in a factory and the sticky stuff turned out to be glue. I can't express how relieved all the girls were."

"I can't imagine," Brooks laughed

When Pam went to bed Brooks stayed out on the deck overlooking the Puget Sound. He removed the crime scene photos from his briefcase and began to review them. He remembered the second story sliding door had not been locked, neither had the front door. That might explain why they didn't find signs of forced entry. He picked up the phone and called the CSPT. He asked if they were still on the scene. Two technicians (techs) were still at the apartment. He asked them to dust both doors for fingerprints and let him know if anything was discovered. He crawled into bed with Pam and fell fast asleep.

The next morning he went to work and the day went by without incident until the Coroner, Jennifer Harris, called with information from the CSPT report and autopsy.

"CSPT found a fingerprint on the victim's sink and hair from the shower drain," Jennifer said. "We received a match on both and I sent a copy to your email inbox. The print returned to a twenty seven year old named Darrel Thompson. Thompson's last known address is at the same apartment complex as the victim. The hair from the shower matched the DNA of Chad Zumwalt. Zumwalt volunteered for the police department and attended numerous trainings through the agency. That's why his DNA came to be on file. Skin recovered from under Zoe's fingernails was sent to the FBI lab because the DNA did not match anyone locally. The DNA will take a few weeks to return."

"They recovered a fingerprint from the sliding glass door on the outside handle," Jennifer continued. "This print didn't match anyone currently in the database, but can be used if a suspect is identified. They also recovered skin from the rope used to tie Zoe. The skin on the rope may be Zoe's, but we can send it to the lab anyway. I didn't find any signs of sexual assault, but recent sexually active is evident. She died from a stab wound to the back that punctured her heart. She bled out quickly and the wound on her back occurred after she died. It's a vertical cut adjoined by a horizontal cut and appears to be the letter L. I can't say conclusively that the cut is a letter or a cut shaped like a letter."

"Mr. Wilkins, your daughter's body is being released for burial," Brooks said to Zoe's parents when he called them back.

Her parents were both distraught and took several minutes to say anything. He could hear Mrs. Wilkins crying and sniffling while Mr. Wilkins tried to comfort her. He regained their attentions.

"One more question," Brooks said. "Did Zoe know anyone named Darrell Thompson or Chad Zumwalt?"

"She'd been dating a guy named Chad for about a year," Zoe's mother replied tearfully. "I don't recall his last name but he is a volunteer police officer. Zoe told us she broke off the relationship, but Chad kept calling her and stopping by to visit her. She was not afraid of him but grew tired of him trying to win her back. The last time I spoke to her a week ago, she told me Chad was at the door and she needed to go."

"Thank you, Mrs. Wilkins," Brooks said. "If you think of anything else, please call me."

CHAPTER 3

In the office the next morning, Cooper and Brooks discussed the new case information.

"We need to research these two and collect as much information as we can before the interviews," commented Brooks.

They began to investigate into the lives of Darrel Thompson and Chad Zumwalt.

Brooks' investigation into Thompson indicated he worked as a part-time maintenance man in the apartment complex where Zoe's murder occurred. He was a 27-year-old man with a shady past. He had several arrests for fighting and assault, as well as drunk driving offenses. Part of his previous sentencing required him to attend anger management, which he successfully completed.

Brooks spoke to the landlord regarding Thompson.

"Thompson began working in the apartment complex three months ago," the landlord said. "And I've received several complaints from female tenants who needed repairs"

"What kind of complaints?" Brooks asked.

"One 25-year-old girl filed the first complaint. She said she told Thompson to wait thirty minutes so she had time to take a shower, but he showed up early and she answered the door in a towel. When she opened the door, Thompson supposedly gave her the elevator eyes, and a sexually suggestive smile. She said that as Thompson fixed the sink, he kept making suggestive comments to her. According to her, Thompson bragged about his sexual skills and he kept rubbing his crotch and suggestively staring at her. He even tried to convince her to go on a date. She threatened to call me and Thompson left."

"Anything else?" Brooks asked.

"Yes, a second complaint came from a 22-year-old female tenant. She said Thompson told her he was supposed to perform scheduled maintenance on the dishwasher. She told him she didn't have a dishwasher in her apartment and Thompson said something about meaning the garbage disposal. She was suspicious but let him in. She said he didn't know how to fix a garbage disposal. He didn't even bring the proper tools. When she mentioned it, Thompson said he brought the right tool for another job he would do for her. She asked Thompson to leave and not come back."

Brooks grimaced. "More?" he asked.

"Yeah, be careful when you contact this guy, he's had martial arts training and he's short tempered."

Brooks requested and received the faxed written complaints.

A computer check for warrants on Thompson indicated an active warrant for assault. Armed with the warrant, Cooper and Brooks prepared to apprehend Thompson.

They contacted the landlord at the apartment complex.

"Where is Thompson now?" asked Cooper.

"He's in apartment 207 unclogging a drain,"

They came to the second story apartment door and made contact with the female occupant.

"Thompson's in the kitchen unclogging the drain," she replied.

"You're under arrest," Brooks and Cooper said as they identified themselves to Thompson.

"I'm not going anywhere," Thompson said aggressively as he reached into his toolbox.

As Cooper stepped towards him, Thompson threw a cleaning solution in his face, temporarily blinding him.

"Oh my God," Cooper screamed in pain and fell to his knees holding his eyes.

Brooks tried to stop Thompson and was kicked in the chest. This knocked Brooks back, but he maintained his feet. He gave chase as Thompson leapt from the balcony of the apartment to the ground below. Thompson hit the ground, rolled, and got up running.

"Son of a bitch," Brooks said.

Brooks called for backup units and gave dispatch Thompson's information and direction of travel. He returned to Cooper who was still in pain and unable to see.

The backup units arrived in the area. Thompson was spotted going into an abandoned two-story building two blocks away. Brooks arrived with additional units and they secured a perimeter around the building. Brooks used the P.A. system in his detective car to call Thompson out of the building.

"Mr. Thompson, we know you are in the building," said Brooks. "You can't get out, you're surrounded. Come out peacefully."

Thompson replied by throwing a brick from the second story through the window of the nearby patrol car smashing the patrol radio. This did not endear the officers to Thompson. Brooks briefed the officers on Thompson's martial arts and assaultive background before entering the building.

"Let's do this by the book," Brooks said. "Start on the bottom floor and work towards the second floor slowly. We don't want this guy to get the upper hand. Besides he may move back downstairs while we're preparing our gear."

Ten officers entered in tactical gear with firearms, Tasers, and beanbag rounds ready for use. Upon entering, the officers immediately smelled the odor of feces, urine and marijuana smoke. They cleared the first floor and encountered several transients squatting in the abandoned building. The transients were quite surprised to be faced with several armed officers and quickly and voluntarily exited the building. On the second floor, the officers slowly moved from room to room. As they approached the end of the hallway, three rooms remained. They cleared the first of the three rooms and found the room empty.

When they entered the second to last room, the officer in the lead was kicked in the helmet. This pushed him back and stopped the momentum of the others following him. They rapidly recovered and cornered Thompson with four officers. His hands were empty and the lead officer with the Taser gave Thompson commands.

"Lie on your stomach and put your hands behind your back," The officer told Thompson.

"I'm not going to jail," Thompson said, refusing the order.

As he yelled, the officer gave him a second order.

"The Taser will be deployed if you do not comply," said the officer. "Lie on the ground and put your hands behind your back"

Thompson continued to refuse the officers orders. The officer targeted high on Thompson's chest and deployed the Taser. One of the two Taser probes struck Thompson in the chest and the other lodged in his tongue. His eyes rolled up in his head as he went stiff before falling on his face, and breaking his nose.

While the chase ensued, Cooper arrived at the hospital and was examined by a doctor.

"Your vision will return in a couple of days," the doctor said as he flushed Cooper's eyes with saline.

This left Brooks to conduct the investigation and interviews alone.

Cooper was being discharged when Thompson arrived at the hospital. Cooper heard Thompson complaining and told Brooks, "Karma's a bitch."

They both laughed. They stayed to see Thompson get his nose reset and the removal of the Taser probes. Thompson decided to be cooperative. He was released into police custody. Still under medication, he was taken to the jail for his warrant. Brooks charged Thompson with assaulting an officer and resisting arrest. His misdemeanor warrant turned into multiple felony charges.

"I'm going to the office and you need to go home," Brooks told Cooper.

Brooks returned to the office to begin researching Chad Zumwalt. Brooks met Zumwalt once at the station but did not know much about him yet.

During his investigation, Brooks discovered Zumwalt had been a volunteer for several local police agencies in the Seattle area, but had been let go because he kept performing police functions without authority. He was a 30-year-old want to be cop who had been a volunteer for Seattle PD for two years. Zumwalt failed some of the tests to become a real officer but maintained hope that he would someday pass.

"His driving record is clean, but his psychological profile indicated that he's more concerned with being labeled a cop than doing the job," Brooks said to himself.

Brooks found that Zumwalt dated several ex-girlfriends who filed stalking complaints against him, but none pressed charges. He had a clear criminal history, and maintained a steady job as a car salesman. He lived with his mother in a small two-bedroom house in a middle class part of town.

Brooks contacted Zumwalt by phone.

"Can you come in for an interview Mr. Zumwalt?" asked Brooks.

"I'll be in at 8 tonight if that works," said Zumwalt. "But why do you need to talk to me?"

Zumwalt sounded nervous when asking why he's being interviewed. His voice cracked, he stuttered and he repeated himself several times.

"We'll talk about it this evening," Brooks assured him.

Zumwalt failed to appear for his interview. Brooks called the residence. Zumwalt's mother informed Brooks that her son left after an earlier phone call upset him.

"Does he have a girlfriend?" Brooks asked.

"I don't know," she replied.

"Where is your son?" he asked again.

"He left and I don't know when he will be back."

Brooks thought she sounded like a man disguising his voice.

CHAPTER 4

Brooks woke early in the morning to a ringing phone. He sleepily answered the phone and was told about a second homicide.

"A woman was found by a college security guard," The dispatcher said. "She has a stab wound and a cut in her back that seems like a letter of the alphabet."

"On my way," Brooks said.

Brooks met the CSPT leader, Angie Jacobson, at the scene. After putting booties on his shoes and gloves on his hands, they entered the scene.

Brooks approached the female victim lying on the ground and noted the stab wound to her back. The woman wore workout clothes like to the other victim. Her hands were tied behind her back with rope similar to the type used on Zoe. The letter A was cut into her shirt and back. The first wound was administered while she stood and the rest were after she lay on the ground. The ground around her was devoid of blood. Brooks deduced the victim bled out somewhere else. He spotted fibers stuck to her workout clothes. Tire tracks in the grass lead up to the body. He asked a tech to get a mold of the tire impressions. He saw a note wadded up in her right hand. After photos were taken of her hand, Brooks removed the paper. The note read, "There's nothing you could do, to save number two. Will you find me, before number three"?

The crime scene tech found an I.D. that indicated she was a 26-year-old student of the college, named Chandra Owens. Chandra's birthday is February of 1988. Brooks asked the campus security guard Nate to access the college computer.

Nate ran off to his office and returned with a small file of information. Brooks discovered Chandra was a third year psychology student who lived in a rental house off campus. Brooks radioed dispatch and asked that a uniformed officer secure her residence. A unit was dispatched to secure the house. Brooks left the scene to the techs and proceeded to the residence.

Chandra arrived home earlier that afternoon. She decided to go to bed early and get a good night sleep. She woke early that morning. She put on her workout clothing and jumped on the spin bike to get a good sweat.

"It's too cold this morning to run outside," she said to herself after seeing the moisture on her window.

Five minutes into her warm-up, she was yanked off her bike knocking it to the ground. Her leg hit the handlebars and they twisted to the side as she came off the bike. She felt someone's hands clamp around her neck and throw her, head first into the mirror. She felt the glass shatter, cutting her head. She fell to the floor, knocking the wind out of her and the attacker immediately picked her up and carried her towards the bedroom. She regained her faculties enough to grab the attacker, scratching his back above his belt. He threw her down on the bed and put all his weight on her back, making it hard for her to breath. She felt the blood in her hair soaking in.

"Put your hands behind your back," he said.

She complied and her hands and feet were tied together.

"I will get off you if you agree not to scream," he said.

She agreed. He picked her up again and carried her back to the exercise room.

"What are you going to do to me?" she asked.

He stood her up facing the broken mirror and stood behind her with his hand on her neck.

"Why do you work out so hard?" he asked.

She began to answer and felt something plunge into her back. She saw her own horrified expression of pain in the broken mirror before collapsing to the floor. She smelled what she thought was metallic and realized it was her blood. The killer left her on the floor of the exercise room while he retrieved the kitchen rug. When he returned, he set the rug aside to ensure Chandra was dead. He began to cut a letter into her back. When he finished he picked her up and set her in the middle of the carpet before rolling her up and taping it closed. He carried her to the sliding glass door and onto the deck. He held her over the rail and dropped her. She landed in the bed of the pickup parked below with a dull thud. He drove her to the college and left her behind a building along the running trail.

***

Brooks entered Chandra's apartment with two officers. He examined a pool of blood in the second room, which appeared to be an exercise room. The blood had dried and looked like dark chocolate in the carpet. The victim's spin bike lay on its side and the handlebars were crooked. The blood pool sat next to a set of weights and a weight machine. He searched the rest of the residence and found no one else. Before leaving he smelled a mixture of perfume and iron. They all exited and Brooks waited for the CSPT.

When they arrived, Brooks walked them through the house. As they entered the kitchen, they noted the center of the wood floor to be darker than the rest of the room. The outside square of the room was sun bleached. This led Brooks to believe that something protected the floor until recently. Upon closer inspection, he saw fibers similar to those found on the body at the scene. He made note of other signs of struggle in the exercise room. The mirror was broken and a small amount of blood remained on it. Brooks left while the techs began to process the scene.

Brooks tried to track down Zumwalt at work and requested he be called to the office. Zumwalt arrived and recognized Brooks.

"I need to take Mr. Zumwalt to the police station for an interview," Brooks told the boss. "Mr. Zumwalt may be a witness to a crime and I need his version of events."

At the station, Zumwalt was put in an interview room, and read his Miranda Rights. Brooks excused himself to get some paperwork for the interview. He returned a little over an hour later apologizing as he entered.

"I was tied up on phone calls," Brooks said.

"I realize it's a common tactic to leave someone in the interview room to get them to talk," Zumwalt said impatiently.

Brooks reminded him of his rights and Zumwalt said he understood. "Are you currently dating anyone?" Brooks asked.

"I recently broke up with my girlfriend, Zoe."

"When's the last time you saw Zoe?"

"We were together a few days ago in her apartment." He explained, "We had breakup sex and both agreed that we would date other people. I

17

took a shower and left around 8:00 PM that night and she was going to run on the treadmill."

"What was she wearing when you left that night?" Brooks asked.

"She always wore a sports bra and her t-shirt with a pair of yoga pants," Zumwalt replied.

"Did you lock the door when you left and was the slider locked?"

"I locked the front door on the way out, but don't remember if the slider was open or shut."

"I am sorry but Zoe's been killed," Brooks informed Zumwalt.

"My mother saw the news and told me," he said without emotion. "It's unfortunate, but I already found a new girl to date."

"Aren't you upset she's dead?" asked Brooks.

"I'm not going to date her again anyway so I haven't lost anything. I am sad but I moved on already" Zumwalt replied callously.

"Where did you go after leaving Zoe's house on the morning of her death?"

"I was doing volunteer hours at the police station until six in the morning on both nights," Zumwalt said.

The interview concluded and Zumwalt returned to work. Brooks reviewed security video of the police station. He found that Zumwalt was telling the truth. He was on video in the station or with another officer both nights.

Brooks called Cooper to ask how he was doing and update him on the case.

"I'll be back to work tomorrow," Cooper said. "I am bored at home and can't wait to get back. I've been bruising my legs on all the furniture because my depth perception is off. I want to get back in the office and help solve the case."

Brooks laughed and said, 'I'll make sure all the office furniture has bumpers so you don't get hurt."

"Screw off," Cooper said and laughed while he hung up.

Brooks completed his paperwork when the captain called him into the office. He dialed Cooper's cell phone and told him to listen.

"Information leaked to the press and they are calling this the Letters of Death case," the captain said. "The chief is pissed that the press has the information about the cases and wants someone's head for leaking it. You are the only one who got all the information that the press reported."

"I have better things to do than talk to the press," Brooks assured the captain. "The crime scene techs and the coroner's office received the same information. If you are going to make accusations you better bring the evidence to back it up."

"Get out of my office and get back to work," the captain ordered.

He walked out and pulled the cell phone from his pocket.

"I heard everything and it's bullshit," Cooper said.

"Why are you surprised?"

"You're right," Cooper said.

"Did you ever hear the case of the rabid dog?" Brooks asked. "The case was a perfect example of their policing skills."

"No," said Cooper.

"Chief Gilmore and Captain Magers were only patrolmen when this happened. You know how the captain always says they never took any lip, and didn't allow any suspects to get the better of them?" Brooks asked.

"Yes," said Cooper.

"They always talk as if they were the best cops who ever did the job," Brooks said. "We both comprehend the chief and captain didn't promote because of their good policing, but rather their ass kissing ability. This case is why the two are more affectionately known by the patrol officers as Jackass and Nimrod," Brooks continued.

"This is what happened. We received a call of a rabid dog chasing people in the city park. We arrived at the park and searched for the dog. The captain saw the dog bolt out from behind a house with foam around his mouth. The captain swung his shotgun in the direction of the dog and fired. He missed the dog but shot the highly dangerous above ground pool. The dog lived that day, but the pool died from internal injuries," Brooks said.

Cooper laughed and ended the call.

Brooks had to wait until the CSPT and Coroner's reports were in and decided to go home.

He arrived home to an empty house. He poured himself a Jack Daniels and Coke, and went out on the back deck overlooking the water. He gazed at the ferryboats crossing from Bremerton to Seattle. It was a calm night with no wind and he felt a sense of peace. Watching the ferry's slowly move back and forth always gave him a sense of serenity.

He started thinking about the case and began to go over his interview notes with Zumwalt. He did not find anything new in the notes and scanned the two sets of photos.

Neither photos showed signs of forced entry. The knots and rope on the wrists were similar and both victims were subdued and tied up prior to being stabbed. The victims wore workout clothing and were in good physical condition. Both sustained a singular stab wound to the back and had a letter cut into them after death.

He asked himself, "Why was the second victim moved from her residence."

The killer wanted her to be found in a timely manner. Did the killer seek publicity or want the victim to be discovered quickly? Brooks was curious what kind of game the killer was playing. He was excellent at games but needed to figure out the rules in order to win this one.

Back in the office the next morning, Brooks went through Chandra Owens' cell phone to contact relatives and to get some background information. He found a number for her mother and made the call. When a female voice answered the phone, Brooks asked, "Are you Chandra's mother?"

"I am."

Brooks identified himself and said, "I am sorry to inform you that your daughter was found deceased yesterday morning."

She began to cry uncontrollably. He heard her lip quivering and a sniffle before she gathered herself. She began to ask questions and Brooks answered what he could.

"I would like to get some information from you when you are able," said Brooks.

"I will call you back," she replied.

After contacting family and her husband, Mrs. Owens called Brooks back.

"I understand this is a difficult time for you and I appreciate you calling me back, Mr. and Mrs. Owens," Brooks said. "I have some questions that will hopefully give me some insight into who your daughter was and how to find the perpetrator in her death."

"I don't understand," Mr. Owens stated.

"Sometimes discussing a person's upbringing and personal history can lead us in the direction of where they may hang out, or what type of people they may associate with. This helps to narrow our investigation and sometimes leads to suspects. If you can give me a brief history of Chandra's life, it might help."

"I understand," said Mr. Owens. "Chandra moved to Seattle four years ago to pursue a career as a personal trainer. She lived on her own the entire time. She dated several young men, but Chandra's more concerned with getting her career started and getting a clientele established."

"The last person Chandra talked about was someone named Bradford, but they haven't been together for a few weeks," her mother said. "Chandra hasn't been dating anyone recently. She moved from Las Vegas to Seattle to get out of the crazy gambling atmosphere and get into one with people that are more active. I am not aware of anyone that would want to harm Chandra and she hadn't been having any trouble."

"Chandra is an avid athlete and works out several hours a day," she said. "She usually runs outside on different paths she found through trial and error. One of her routes goes by the college and she talked about how beautiful the trails through the campus are. She loved the pine trees and the fresh flower smells on the trail."

She began crying again. "I'm sorry."

"I think that's enough for now," Mr. Owens said.

"Thank you for the information. I will do everything I can to find who did this to your daughter," Brooks said and concluded the conversation.

The coroner's report and the crime scene tech's reports arrived while Brooks was on the phone. He was not the first to read them. Cooper came in after his injury time off and wanted to get back into the case.

Cooper began to read the coroner's report with red sore eyes. Jennifer reported that Zoe suffered bruising on her neck and back from being struck from behind. She also showed signs of defensive bruises on her hands as if she fought back and punched something. Rope fibers were imbedded in the skin around her wrist and she suffered rope burns. She had a small cut on her right wrist and broke her thumb while freeing her left hand from the binding. Zoe had a small abrasion on the front of her neck. Jennifer speculated that the killer held the knife against her neck to gain her compliance. She wrote that the marks on her neck were consistent with the type of knife that made the entry wound in her back.

The stab wound had been administered while she stood and punctured the center of her heart. A cut in her back formed the letter L. She probably collapsed immediately after the initial wound and the remaining wounds occurred while she lay on the ground unable to resist. The stab wound was deep and precise while the following cuts were shallow and only broke through ¼-inch layer of skin. Zoe had been dead within minutes of the initial stab wound. Zoe did not show any signs of sexual assault but had been sexually active recently. Jennifer found sweat on the neck and back of her workout clothes.

Jennifer found skin under Zoe's fingernails that was not her own. She sent the samples to the crime lab and the results would return in a couple weeks. Jennifer also found fibers on Zoe that did not match the clothing she wore or the carpet samples taken from her apartment. They were examined at the lab and would be in the crime scene report.

Cooper read the crime scene reports. Hair was found in the shower drain, and blood stained the towels on the floor of Zoe's bathroom. They had been able to use an alternate light source (ALS) and found some boot impressions. They used plastic film to get a clear imprint of the wear patterns. The impression was uploaded to the FBI database for comparison. Within an hour, they received a match. The boots were a size 11 Pro-tech with distinct wear patterns on the big toe area and on the inside of the heel. This indicated that the wearer over pronated or rotated inward towards the inside of the foot while walking. They found fingerprints on the hand rail outside the second story sliding glass door that were a match to the fingerprints taken from the slider, but didn't match the print on the sink. The fingerprint on the sink matched to a Darrell Thompson.

CHAPTER 5

Except for the tire impressions, the second crime scene at the college only revealed evidence recovered from the victim's body. The fibers Brooks noted were collected, as well as the skin under the victim's nails. These fibers were not a match to the fibers taken from the victim's carpet. However, they did match the fibers found in the kitchen. When compared to fibers in the database they matched a generic carpet sold in outlet stores across the country. The carpet had been manufactured from 1988 through 2000 and used in a nylon brown throw rug that shed over time. The carpet was most commonly manufactured as a six by nine foot floor carpet. This was consistent with the size of unbleached flooring Brooks detected on the wood floor in Chandra's apartment.

The coroner's report on Chandra indicated she scratched the suspect, leaving his skin under her nails. The DNA profile of the skin matched the DNA found on the first victim, but still didn't match anyone in the local database. Both samples were sent to the FBI lab for further comparison. This victim had been stabbed in the back puncturing her heart and the letter A cut into her. The stab and cuts were consistent with the previous victim.

The CSPT reported that the apartment of the second victim revealed little more. Inside the apartment, they were able to get another set of boot impressions that matched the first victim's apartment. They extracted a DNA sample from the blood on the broken mirror in the exercise room, which was later determined to be Chandra's blood. The second scene was a little different from the first. The victim was carried to and from the bedroom during the attack. The rope fibers indicated she was tied up in the bedroom and brought back to the exercise room to be killed. They deduced the killer was male and the DNA later confirmed that fact. It took a tremendous amount of strength to subdue and carry someone of her size and weight. Chandra had been 5 foot 9 and weigh 140 pounds. That amount of weight is not easy to carry. CSPT reported that the fibers at the college scene didn't match the remaining carpets at the apartment.

As Cooper completed reading the reports, Brooks entered. Brooks walked to the coffee machine and then came over to his desk. Cooper knew not to talk to him until about half a cup of coffee surged through his blood. He waited a few minutes for the coffee to do its job before he began to brief Brooks on the reports.

When Brooks was in high school, a local gym owner approached him.

"Would you like an opportunity to train at the boxing academy?" a local gym owner asked Brooks.

"I can't afford it," Brooks said.

"How about if I let you clean the gym after school and we call it even," the gym owner offered.

"That sounds cool," said Brooks.

Brooks began to train hard. He used his family and life frustrations as motivators in the ring and excelled quickly. Within a few years, he dominated the heavy weights and went on to win the golden gloves boxing championship. He worked for Seattle PD for the past 30 years and used his skills several times. He had witnessed a lot in his career and rarely witnessed anything new. Cooper was the only one who had knowledge of Brooks' fighting skills.

"I am so glad I didn't go to the drug task force," Cooper said. "I would have missed out on this case. This may possibly put us both in the homicide squad."

"Don't sound so excited about these murders," Brooks replied.

"I know this doesn't sound good, but I think if we make the homicide squad, we can make a big difference in solving cases," he retorted.

He and Brooks focused back on the case. They feared that another murder was not far away. If the pattern continued, they wouldn't make it through the next day or two without another homicide.

While reviewing the evidence, they were summoned to the chief's office ASAP. They made their way to his office and were met by the secretary.

"The press has been calling all morning and the chief is pissed off," she warned them.

They entered the chief's office with the warning in mind. The chief asked them to sit.

"I have to hold a press conference to inform the media about the case and to warn young women about suspicious characters." The chief said.

"You'll be attending the conference with me."

"Why," They asked.

"I appointed you to a task force to get this case solved quickly. You'll serve as the lead detectives in the case. You'll also be appointed an evidence technician to assist you. You are no longer on patrol and will focus solely on what the media is calling the Letters of Death case."

"We need to get to the press conference," the chief said as he stood up. "I will tell you what to say on the way down.

He further instructed as the elevator bounced, "Tell the media only the names and ages and of the victims and that any further information will not be released to protect the integrity of the investigation."

During the press conference, the chief announced the appointment of the two veteran officers as lead detectives in a task force that he formed to focus on the case.

"I appointed two other staff to the task force but don't want to divulge those member's names or areas of expertise," said the chief.

Cooper and Brooks understood that this would allow the chief to move or change the other members of the task force at will.

After the press conference, the chief informed Brooks and Cooper they would now be working out of a separate office that only task force members can access, but would still use all the resources of the police department. This meant that Cooper and Brooks would be working out of the old sex crimes offices that combined with the burglary division years ago. They were on the same floor as the administration and felt they would not be the only ones with access to the office. The two spent the rest of the day moving all their equipment into the new offices and getting computers and phones set up for the new task force hot lines. They also met the two other members assigned to the task force. One member was Angie from CSPT, and the other was the head coroner, Jennifer. The four had known each other for years and got along well.

Angie was an attractive 38-year-old woman who worked in the department for the past ten years and was an exceptional evidence technician. She worked all types of cases, was thorough and able to process a crime scene to the smallest detail. Angie grew up in the Puget Sound area and always knew she wanted to serve the community. She lived with an abusive stepfather and her mother. Angie originally wanted to work as a domestic violence counselor. When she entered high school, she began to play sports and lettered in tennis. She attended a high school party during her first year and her drink was spiked. While unconscious, she had been raped. This event changed her career goals. Angie decided to study forensic science to help convict the type of people she dealt with in her personal life.

***

The chief came into the office at the end of the day and informed them, "I wanted to let you know Jennifer and Angie will only be task force members when their expertise is needed, the rest of the time they will perform their normal job assignments. We don't have enough resources in those departments to spare them on a full time basis"

They were not surprised by this announcement, but it would still only give the task force part-time resources.

"You get the next two days to go over the evidence and reports," the chief said. "That time will be extended if more homicides occur."

The day ended without another homicide.

CHAPTER 6

In the morning, the newly formed task force arrived in their office and began a briefing on the case.

"How did the killer get into the women's apartments?" asked Brooks.

Maybe he's a cable installer or building inspector," said Cooper. "It has to be someone who can get in and out of an apartment without being questioned."

"He may be coming in the sliding glass door," said Angie. "You know most people with second story apartments leave the slider open."

Everyone held their breath when the new phone rang.

Cooper answered the phone and began to write information down. At the conclusion of the call, he told the team they needed to go and would brief them on the way.

"Another body has been discovered in an apartment." Cooper said. "This time it's a 28-year-old woman. The apartment manager scheduled a walk-through with a new tenant. When the tenant failed to answer the door, he entered to do the walk-through without her. He found his tenant on the floor of the bedroom with a stab wound in her back."

Before her death, Ashley Long had a quiet morning. She began the day with a healthy banana to fuel up for her five-mile bike ride. She hoped to beat her time from yesterday. She put on her workout clothes and headed out the door. Half way through her ride, she questioned whether she'd locked her front door. She returned from her workout and prepared for a shower. She sat on the bed and removed her shoes and socks. As she put the second sock on her shoe, someone rushed out of her closet and pinned her to the bed.

"Put your hands behind your back," the attacker demanded as he held a knife to her throat.

She put her hands behind her back.

"If you scream I will cut your throat," he told her. She complied and her hands were tied behind her back. The perpetrator flipped her onto her back and began to pull her shorts down. She tried to kick him and he again showed her the knife.

"If you comply, I won't hurt you," he lied.

He pulled down her shorts and lifted her sports bra. He raped her while she laid in terror. When the assault was over, she flipped onto her stomach to protect herself. She felt a sense of hope as the attacker moved off the bed to leave, until the knife penetrated her back. She felt blood gushing out, felt sick to her stomach and soon everything went black. The attacker calmly cleaned his knife in the bathroom before ensuring that Ashley was dead. He made several cuts in her back. The first being vertical, followed by a connecting diagonal cut, and finally another vertical cut parallel to the first, forming a letter. After searching around her apartment, he walked out the door as if nothing happened.

***

The team arrived at the scene and asked the landlord to tell them where he'd walked and what rooms he'd entered. They also requested he write down every action he took while inside the apartment. Angie put her booties and gloves on to examine the scene with the CSPT. During the initial entry into the apartment, Angie found the woman's purse with an ID.

"The victim's 28-year-old Ashley Long. She was born in March of 1986," Angie said.

The team moved slowly from room to room examining everything as they went. When Angie entered the bathroom, she discovered blood drops that lead from the bathroom to the bedroom. CSPT examined the kitchen. They noted silverware scattered throughout the room and disheveled countertops.

The team gathered in the hall outside the bedroom door. They stood at the door for a moment to take an overview of the scene. Before moving into the room, Angie took photos to prove what existed prior to the investigation. Each member of the team knew to take photos before entering a room as well as photographing evidence in place before removing it. She smelled an odor that only comes when a dead persons bowels release. She tried to cover her nose to no avail.

Angie photographed and measured the distance from a fixed point to the evidence and took close-ups of the collected items. This would enable the team to reconstruct the scene, down to the smallest piece of evidence.   Once the room had been completed, CSPT focused on the body.

The victim wore athletic gear and appeared as if she returned from a run when she was killed. She wore a form fitted shirt with spandex shorts, and a sports bra. An IPOD was found in a pocket of the shorts with music still playing.

"Batteries only last eight hours with the music running," Angie said. "So the homicide occurred within that time. The landlord called almost two hours ago. That narrows the time of death even more. Jennifer will be able to give a more accurate time during the autopsy."

Ashley lay face down on the floor with her hands tied behind her back. Her feet were tied together with the same burlap type of rope as the other victims. She had one visible stab wound, and several cuts forming the letter N in her back. It appeared as if she walked to the bedroom before being stabbed. They discovered three sets of footprints on the hall carpet and one belonged to the landlord. They assumed the suspect and victim walked to the bedroom together.

They turned Ashley over and discovered something different.

"Ashley's shorts are pulled down and appear to contain semen on the front of them," said Angie. "Her sports bra is pulled up exposing her breasts."

"This is strange," said Brooks. "A suspect doesn't usually go from homicide, to rape and homicide. This is not a normal progression of violence. We are dealing with a truly twisted individual. A rapist may eventually murder, but a killer doesn't typically start raping. This is the first time I've heard of this progression in reverse. This isn't good."

"She's got a note in her hand," said Angie.

She photographed Ashley's hand and removed the note. The paper read, "You couldn't stop me before number 3. You'll have to do more to catch me before number four."

Angie left the Crime Scene Processing Team to process for fingerprints and any other evidence.

After the team completed the scene, Ashley's body was taken to the coroner for further exam.   Jennifer accompanied Ashley's body to the morgue and scrubbed up to perform the autopsy. She awaited the arrival of the rest of the task force before beginning her procedure. Upon their arrival, she began. She initiated the process by examining the body with a high-powered microscope, which showed the images on an 80-inch television screen for easy viewing.

Jennifer located several fibers from Ashley's body, which appeared to match the carpet in her apartment. She scraped under Ashley's fingernails, which had been clipped and recently cleaned. Jennifer removed the victims clothing to examine them for DNA. She recovered DNA from the shorts to be sent to the FBI crime lab. Jennifer washed the victim's body with purified water. Everything that rinsed off is caught in a microscopic filter that can be further examined at the crime lab for new evidence.

"Ashley was raped prior to her death," Jennifer said. "She was stabbed in the back once and had the letter N cut in her back. The initial stab punctured her heart while she lay down. I was able to deduce the time of death to between 4 am and 6 am. These stab wounds were administered with surgical precision."

"How can you calculate the time of death," Angie asked.

"Time of death is a calculation based off the body temperature, the temperature of the room where the body is located, levels of rigor mortis or decay, and several other factors," Jennifer replied.

After completing the autopsy, the team met in their offices to go over the case. It appeared the suspect was fond of athletic, attractive woman in the twenties, who lived alone in apartments.

"I'll do the background check on Ashley and bring the information to the team to check for any connection between victims," Cooper stated.

During Cooper's investigation, he discovered that Ashley was an only child whose parents passed away. She was born in March of 1986. He was unable to locate any surviving members of her family. He discovered her parents were severe drug addicts in her early teens and she lived on her own since the age of 16. Her mother died of a drug overdose five years ago and her father committed suicide on the first anniversary of his wife's death.

Ashley had been a student at the college and she graduated with a degree in physical education. She studied to be a physical education teacher for developmentally disabled children. He also discovered that she owned a green Honda Accord registered to her that wasn't at the scene. He put out a BOLO, or Be On the Look Out, for the vehicle.

Cooper filled out administrative warrants for cell phone companies who provided service to the area. This would allow the cell service provider to tell him if the victims were clients. He would fill out a search warrant for all records pertaining to the victim's accounts and only serve the specific providers. If Ashley owned a cell phone, the team would compare all three victim's numbers for a common link.

Cooper briefed the team. They compared case notes and discovered all three victims attended the local university. All the victims were at least 5 foot 7, Caucasian, attractive, physically fit and living in apartments.

"I'll get the college records and find out if the victims had any professors, students, janitors or other employees in common while attending school," Brooks said. "Jennifer is going to compare the autopsy reports for any similarities."

"Angie and I will go over the evidence and reports while you two are busy," said Cooper. "We can meet in the morning to share what information we uncover."

Brooks arrived at the college and spoke to the Dean of the college. The Dean agreed to make copies of all school records for the three students including registration rosters for each victim's classes and the professor's names. After about three hours, Brooks received all the paperwork. In the morning, the team would scour throughout the paperwork for connections.

CHAPTER 7

The phone rang when Brooks arrived home. Fearing another homicide occurred, he answered. He was pleasantly surprised to hear his daughter's voice.

"Mom and I are coming to visit you for Christmas if you don't have plans," Lexi said.

"That would be fantastic. I would love to see you both," he quickly exclaimed.

Lexi caught him up on the last month of her life and Brooks did the same, not mentioning the current case.

"How's your mother doing?" he asked.

"Here she is," handing off the phone.

Brooks spoke to his ex-wife Janet. She immediately recognized that something troubled him. She always detected his mood with a word or two. He told her briefly about the case and expressed his concern for what may happen before the case is solved.

"I know you're the best cop for the job and you will not give in until the public is safe," Janet assured. "You don't stop until you sink your fangs into the suspect and put them behind bars."

He laughed and talked to both women for about an hour. He hung up the phone with a sense of excitement and anticipation of seeing Lexi and Janet in a few weeks. He began to clean the spare room. He straightened the comforter and checked for dust on the furniture. He laughed at himself for acting as if they would arrive tomorrow.

He sat in his favorite chair gazing at the water. Before he realized, the morning light crept through his windows. He'd slept better than he had in months, knowing he was going to see his two favorite women.

Jennifer, Angie, and Cooper were already in the office when Brooks arrived. He put a stack of papers on the desk and assigned one victim's file to each member of the team. They began by comparing professors of all three victims and none matched. The janitorial and security staff's quick turn over meant they hadn't worked with all three victims. Next, they went over the student registration rosters. This would take hours.

They brought the coffee pot into the conference room and reloaded their caffeine for a long day.

After four hours, they did not find a common link. They took a break and headed to lunch.

"Do you guys remember what happened last time we were here?" asked Brooks.

They all thought about the incident in silence.

In September of the same year, a man walked into the restaurant while they were eating and attempted to rob the host at the cash register. None of the four were in uniform at the time and were not identifiable as police department employees. Cooper gestured to Brooks and he perceived what was happening. Cooper walked towards the bathroom past the register as if he didn't understand what was going on. Brooks headed to the bar counter by the register. To get to the bathroom Cooper would need to walk behind the suspect and that would give him a chance to make his move.

Brooks became aware of the suspect holding his hand in his jacket as if he held a gun. He signaled this to Cooper. Cooper headed towards the front door and the register. When he was about ten feet away, the host handed the money over and the suspect ran out the door while Cooper and Brooks gave chase. Angie called 911 and told dispatch that two plains clothes officers were in pursuit of a robbery suspect from their location. She described the suspect and what Cooper and Brooks were wearing.

The suspect ran to the right before turning down an alley. Brooks thought the suspect was unaware he was being chased. They turned the corner to the alley and caught sight of the suspect squatting down, stuffing the money in his inside jacket pocket. When the suspect spotted them, he again began to run. Cooper identified himself as a police officer and they continued to run after the thief. The suspect turned left at the end of the alley, with the two officers gaining on him.

When the two rounded the corner where the suspect turned, they saw that he stopped and assumed a shooting stance forty feet away. Cooper dove to the right and in front of a parked car while drawing his duty weapon. Brooks did a tuck and roll into a brick entryway and drew his weapon. They again identified themselves as police and instructed the suspect to drop his weapon and get on the ground. The suspect remained in his shooting stance and began to slowly move toward them. They gave him several commands to drop his weapon and lay on the ground. The suspect stood 30 feet away and began to raise his gun towards Cooper. Cooper and Brooks both fired twice and hit him each time. The suspect went down but retained his weapon. While behind cover Brooks grabbed his cell phone and updated dispatch where they were and what happened.

They continued to give the suspect commands to drop his weapon. He refused the commands and raised the gun up at them. They stayed behind cover. Brooks told the suspect that if he dropped the weapon they would assist him and render aid. The suspect refused and attempted to fire at Brooks. He became too weak to hold the gun and aim. The shot hit a car ten feet from the suspect and nowhere near the two officers. Both maintained their positions until the suspect became unresponsive and couldn't lift the gun. Cooper and Brooks approached, tactically moving from cover to cover until they were close enough to remove the weapon from the suspect's hand. Brooks placed the gun in his waistband until he secured it in his vehicle for evidence.

After hand cuffing the suspect and searching him for further weapons they radioed for medics and the Shooting Response Team (SRT). Cooper checked the suspect for a pulse and did not find one. They attempted to administer first aid to the best of their ability. The suspect was hit once in the pelvis, once in the right collarbone, once in the torso and one round went through his non-shooting arm and into his chest. The medics arrived and the suspect was taken to Harborview Medical Center for treatment, but died on arrival. Four members of the SRT arrived. Two remained at the scene to investigate and interview witnesses and two transported Cooper and Brooks to interview rooms for statements.

Once in separate interview rooms, they were both read their rights and asked to relay the events of the day to the SRT interrogator. Cooper and Brooks relayed the events of their lunch hour to the respective investigators and were released. They were advised they would be placed on administrative leave for a minimum of ten days. They would attend mandatory counseling during that time before being cleared for duty. When they returned to duty, they were told that the Shooting Response Team would be investigating further. Both would continue counseling and a Coroner's Inquest would be necessary. The shooting occurred three months ago and they were still waiting for the outcome of the investigation.

The SRT investigation, through eyewitness accounts, determined that the shooting was justified and they were allowed to continue working. The suspect had been a known thief and robbed six stores within his last two weeks. His name was Jonathon Malcom, age 48. John had been suspected of numerous robberies and was known to carry a weapon. His record showed several assault charges. John's fingerprints were compared to open cases in the criminal database. The computer came back with numerous hits for felony burglary, and one attempted homicide, in which John had been in a home and encountered the homeowner. John shot the homeowner, who survived, but was unable to ID her attacker at the time. Cooper and Brooks felt better about taking a career criminal off the streets, but recognized that they would have some issues to deal with in taking a human life. Both these men were involved in fatal shootings before, but were not so hardened that this incident would not affect them.

This reminded Cooper of another shooting. During his fourth year as a patrol officer, Cooper made a routine traffic stop that resulted in the death of the driver and a bullet wound to his own arm. The driver jumped out of the car, and began to shoot at Cooper. He returned fire while moving to cover. During the gunfight, a bullet struck Cooper in the upper left arm barely missing his brachial artery. The suspect had been hit several times. When the suspect went down and the threat over, Cooper realized he had been hit. He was cleared in the shooting by the Shooting Response Team weeks later.

He struggled with the knowledge he killed another human being. He sought counseling for the incident and returned to full duty after his physical therapy concluded. Upon returning, Cooper picked up where he left off. He was now 25 years into his career handling the case that may well give him the position he always wanted. Cooper was regularly recruited by the drug task force, and to be a field-training officer, but he held out for a special assignment in the homicide squad. If they solved this case, it might lead to a permanent assignment in his dream position.

After reminiscing over lunch, the task force returned to the conference room. They resumed their work, but Angie and Jennifer couldn't forget the shooting.

They completed the comparison of all three girls and found five students who attended classes with the three victims. The students ranged in age from 25-45 years old. Each team member agreed to take a name from the list in the morning to investigate with a fine-toothed comb.

That evening they decided to meet for a drink. They discussed how they felt while the shooting investigation continued. The team wasn't concerned about any evidence that would indicate the shooting was not justified, but at the same time, they weren't making the decision.

"How do you feel about taking a human life?" Angie asked. "Never mind, let's go to Cooper's and make a drink. It's getting too busy and loud in here."

The two men were stoic about the incident until they had a couple of drinks.

"We had no choice that day," said Brooks. "We did what we were trained to do. We protected ourselves, and the citizens on the street. The shooting was justified, and I won't lose any sleep. Besides, I have a case to focus on."

The two women realized these men were not that cold-hearted and would deal with the aftermath of the incident at some point. They also understood that Brooks and Cooper were focused on the case and didn't choose to think about the shooting.

"I did have several dreams about the incident in the past few months," Brooks said. "I kept dreaming that the suspect gave up and was arrested without incident. That would have been a better outcome for everyone."

"I kept going over the incident in my mind trying to find a different way to end it," Cooper said. "I've gone over the shooting a thousand times but couldn't come up with another way to resolve it."

"I understand we did what we were trained to do, but still wish the suspect had not forced us to protect ourselves with deadly force," Cooper continued. "I think of the shooting quite often and rerun the scenarios through my head, second-guessing our actions, even though we know we did the right thing."

"That's true," agreed Brooks.

Jennifer and Angie understood how these two men were able to be so calm after discussing the incident again, when they realized Brooks and

Cooper had more than 50 years of experience and were involved in this type of incident several times. They were glad they had not experienced what these men went through. As the conversation went on, Angie began to feel an attraction towards Brooks. He's the alpha male of alpha males and didn't appear to let anything faze him. Even after a few drinks, he kept his faculties in check and stopped drinking so he would remain sharp in case someone needed him. Angie only drank one drink and agreed to give the two men a ride home.

The three arrived at Cooper's house.

"Come in for a drink," Cooper said.

"Okay, but we can't stay long," said Brooks.

"I don't want anything, thanks," said Angie. "I still have to drive home and get Brooks home."

The three briefly talked about the task force case and then Brooks announced, "I am going to arrange for my ex-wife and daughter to come over for the Christmas holiday."

Angie showed surprise that he would invite his ex-wife to stay with him. He explained the relationship with her and that she stayed in a spare room, Angie seemed relieved. He found her response interesting but wasn't sure he read her correctly. After the two men consumed another drink, they all decided to go home and get a good night's sleep to start fresh in the morning. They lost part of the day today talking about the past shooting.

When they arrived at Brooks' house, Angie asked if she could use his restroom before heading home. He invited her in and directed her to where she needed to go. He opened the slider, sat in a chair on the deck to view the ferryboats on the water and let out a heavy sigh.

"That sounded like you released the stress of the day." Angie said when she came out on the deck.

"It relaxes me to sit out here and breathe the fresh air while I stare out at the movement on the water," Brooks replied. "Take a seat and appreciate the view for yourself."

Within minutes, he gazed over and saw her sound asleep. Brooks went inside and straightened up the spare room. He woke Angie up.

"You're welcome to use the guest room," Brooks said.

"I don't want anyone at work to think something is going on and I'm okay to drive," she stated with concern.

"I am not going to tell anyone and you'll come back in the morning and get me anyway."

"On the condition that no one knows I spent the night," she agreed. "Since I don't need to drive I can stay up with you a while."

Angie began to tell Brooks about a case she worked.

"The case involved an elderly couple named Fred and Peggy who ran a bed and breakfast in Olympia, Washington. Fred disappeared and Peggy never reported him missing. Their children came to visit and Peggy said Fred ran off. The children didn't believe their father would do that and reported him missing. Once the report appeared on the news, several neighbors reported Peggy burying something in the back yard weeks earlier. The police served a warrant on the property and found the bones of Fred."

She continued, "CSPT had been called in and they thought all the muscles had been stripped from the bones before being buried. CSPT began to process the B and B. What they discovered was appalling."

"Peggy made all the meals for the residents of the B and B. During the CSPT processing, they found blood on the sausage maker and meat grinder. The DNA from the blood came back a match to Fred. Peggy was arrested for murder. She ultimately confessed to killing her husband, chopping him up, and serving him to the travelers staying at the B and B as breakfast sausage. She admitted to burying the bones in the yard, and said she hated Fred's attitude."

Brooks gazed at Angie with an appalled expression and said, "On that note I am going to bed."

CHAPTER 8

Angie woke in the morning to the smell of fresh coffee brewing. As she entered the living room, she spotted Brooks on the deck peering out over the water. He wore only a pair of shorts. He was well toned and in terrific shape for a man his age. She spotted several scars on his back and one long scar on his leg that she knew occurred on the job. She went to the kitchen and filled a coffee cup Brooks set out for her. She saw Brooks walking back in and he seemed shocked to see her.

He stuttered and said, "Sorry for my attire, I'm not used to having company." As he walked by she glimpsed how well built he was. She thought after the case ended she may come and have a drink in private and see where it led. Angie shook her head to clear it and realized she needed to get ready for work.

On the way to the office the two didn't speak except when she again said, "Don't mention that I spent the night."

"Don't worry I won't," he said.

They separated when they arrived at the office. He went directly to his desk and she came in ten minutes later wearing different clothes than she wore in the car. He eyeballed her quizzically and she said she always has extra clothes nearby.

The two others arrived and they convened in the conference room. Each took a name to investigate. Cooper took Howard Jenkins and began digging. He found that Jenkins was 26 and graduated in May. Howard had been arrested once for DUI in high school but nothing since. He had been a straight A student and attended classes with all three girls. Cooper spoke to several of Howard's professors and each said he was a good student and seemed focused on his education.

Cooper contacted Howard and found that he had been working out of state since graduation. He asked Howard to provide copies of check stubs from his job and his boss' phone number. Howard faxed the information. Howard's boss called within 15 minutes and verified that he worked in the oil fields in North Dakota every day for the last six months.

Jennifer investigated the name Jeremy Shumacher, age 25. She found that Jeremy also graduated in May, but still lived in the area. He had a clear criminal history, but, at age 22, had been questioned in a theft. She spoke to several of his professors and found that he was an average student.

"Jeremy had trouble in social situations and seemed shy and introverted," one professor said. "He never talked to or interacted with any other students in class."

When Jennifer called Jeremy's phone number a woman answered.

She asked for Jeremy and the woman defensively asked, "Who's calling?"

She identified herself and the woman said she would get Jeremy. Jennifer spoke to Jeremy and she discovered that he lived with his mom and worked as a parking lot attendant at the new football stadium.

"I also work as a bartender at the DD strip club," he stated.

"Do you know the girls who were killed?"

"I didn't," he replied.

"You registered for at least one class with each of them," Jennifer said.

"I didn't talk to anyone in my classes," he stated.

"Where were you on the nights the girls were killed?" she continued.

"I was at work at the club," he explained. "I'll even provide my timecards as proof."

"An officer will come by the club to talk to your boss and anyone who can verify your whereabouts on the nights in question," she informed him.

"That's fine," he said and gave her all the information she requested.

By noon the next day, she received his time cards and a patrol officer took written statements from his coworkers and employer verifying his whereabouts on the nights in question.

While Cooper and Jennifer were out of the room doing their investigation, Brooks walked to the coffee machine and asked Angie, "Is it hot in here?"

"I don't think so," she said.

"It sure was nice sleeping together last night," he replied.

She immediately scanned around the room to see if anyone heard and turned crimson red.

"Now is it hot in here?" he asked, not expecting an answer.

She stared at him and shook her head, saying with a smile, "Payback's a bitch."

Brooks returned to his work and began his investigation on 45-year-old Luther Jackson. Jackson had been arrested once for possession of marijuana and had numerous speeding tickets. Brooks contacted Jackson.

"Mr. Jackson, did you know any of the girls?" asked Brooks.

"I think I had a class with one or two of them but I'm an older student and don't associate with those kids," Jackson said. "I remember having a science class with Zoe, but I'm not sure about the others."

"Have you seen any of them lately?" Brooks asked.

"I haven't," Jackson replied.

"Where were you on the nights of the murders?"

Jackson became defensive and yelled, "Am I a suspect?"

"We need to talk to everyone who attended classes with the girls. We want to rule out as many people as we can so the focus of the investigation continues in the right direction."

This seemed to calm Jackson and he reported, "I am in Texas with my family at a funeral. My cousin passed away suddenly last week. I kept hotel receipts and flight information if you need them. We will not return until next week."

"Thank you for your cooperation Mr. Jackson," Brooks said as he ended the call.

Angie finally cooled off from Brooks' little surprise statement and began to investigate 30-year-old Marvin Deltin. Deltin had an extensive criminal record beginning in high school. He had been arrested for being a peeping tom. He progressed to an arrest for breaking and entering into a single woman's home. He was charged with rape and served almost a year in jail. Six months after his release he committed a second rape and attempted murder, but the charges were dropped when the witness moved out of state and refused to testify. Deltin is a registered sex offender.

Angie was aware that sex offenders are required to submit up-to-date information on file with the local police. She requested a copy of his sex offender registration and received it in her email. She thought this made him a prime candidate to be their killer. According to Deltin's school registration, he took mostly night classes to get his degree. About 75 percent of his classes were at night. Deltin eventually stopped attending and never completed his degree. She contacted Deltin at the number listed for his home, identified herself and the reason for her call.

Deltin became suspicious and immediately defensive, "The only reason you're calling me is my record. If you want to talk to me, you need go through my attorney. I was already railroaded by the police once, and it isn't going to happen again," he ended.

She tried to ask who his attorney is, but he already hung up.

Angie circled his name and underlined it several times as a prime suspect. She couldn't wait to tell the rest of the team what she encountered but they were all currently on the phone with their own investigations.

Deltin reminded her of what happened to her in high school. Because of that incident in high school, she lost her way. Angie began to drink and use recreational drugs in order to forget all the negative things that happened to her in life. By the end of her senior year, her mother gave Angie an ultimatum to find a job or plan on going to college.

Angie refocused on the case and proceeded to the final name on the list, Darius Farmer, age 29. She began her investigation but it ended as quickly as it started. The school records indicated that Darius stopped attending classes mid-semester. The college later discovered Darius died in a motorcycle accident. Angie confirmed this information with police records and crossed him off the list.

"We need to hold a briefing before the end of the day," Angie told the team. "I may have a break in the case and want to let everyone know before we leave."

She continued to research Deltin and found that his DNA was not in the database even though he had been arrested for rape. She found that he reported to a Probation Officer (PO) for two years after his release on the rape charge. She contacted his PO and found that Deltin failed to maintain a steady job and moved every couple of months while on probation.

"I no longer have current information for Deltin," the PO told her. "I firmly believe that Deltin is a high-risk to reoffend. Deltin always blamed the victims for his behavior and never took responsibility for his actions. At one of our meetings Deltin admitted that he didn't get the type of satisfaction he expected while committing the rape," the PO continued, "he told me he expected to get a better rush from the rapes than he had been getting. I recommended Deltin for mandatory counseling before being released from parole, but due to budget cuts, the counseling was not approved."

"I appreciate the information, you were a huge help," Angie told the PO.

Angie felt excited now. This is an excellent lead, and may be the break that solves this case. The team settled into the conference room. When Angie entered, she relayed all the information she uncovered. Everyone on the team seemed to get renewed energy.

CHAPTER 9

All four members of the team had trouble sleeping in light of the new information. When they arrived at the office the next morning, they printed a copy of Deltin's driver's license. Angie dispersed the photo among the squad meetings.

Being a registered sex offender, Deltin is required by law to give the local law enforcement agency any change of address, phone number or any other means to contact him. He's also required to list his current job and notify the agency when any of his information changed. Angie attempted to contact Deltin again, but his home phone was no longer in service. She attempted to verify the information on his registration form, but none of it was current. Deltin failed to register current information as a sex offender.

Based on the new information, the team applied for an arrest warrant and gave instructions to the patrol units to arrest him upon contact. They also requested to be notified when Deltin was in custody.

The team spent the day trying to track Deltin through vehicle registrations, driver's licensing, home purchases, or any other public records searches they had access to, until they built probable cause for a search warrant of other records.

Shortly after lunch, the task force received a call that another body had been found. Officers secured the scene and were awaiting their arrival.

"The victim had been found by her boyfriend when he came to take her out for dinner," said the dispatcher. "She's in her twenties, attractive, athletic, and living alone, in a second story apartment with a sliding glass door to the alley. Her name's Janelle Phoenix."

Janelle had been in a wonderful mood that morning. She planned a date with her boyfriend to celebrate their six-month anniversary together. This was her longest relationship so far and she loved Steve. Her energy level was high when she headed out the door for a run. She ran farther today than ever before. She felt so excited. As she took her shoes off for a shower, she couldn't stop smiling. She put her shoes and socks at the foot of the bed and went to the closet to pick out her clothes for after the shower. As she opened the closet, a stranger rushed out and pinned her to the bed. He quickly put a knife to her throat.

"If you cooperate, I won't kill you," he told her.

"What do you want? How did you get in here?" she tearfully asked.

"You should lock your doors when you leave darling," he said. "I need you to turn over and put your hands behind your back."

"No, don't tie me up please," she pleaded.

He grabbed both her hands and pinned them to the bed. He put his head down on her abdomen and bit her above the navel. She cried out in pain.

"I won't ask again," he said angrily.

She complied and turned over, placing her hands behind her back. He tied her hands together and turned her back over. He proceeded to rape her while threatening her with the knife. She mentally disassociated with the current events and he spotted a glazed expression on her face. When he finished he got up off the bed.

"You got what you wanted now leave," she said with new resolve.

"I leave on my terms," he said.

He turned her over and angrily plunged the knife down into her. She tried to scream but didn't have any air. She passed out from the pain. She bled out in minutes. Once her life ended, he used his knife to cut an oval into her back, on her left shoulder blade. Janelle would not live to the six-month anniversary date. The killer removed a note pad from his pocket and wrote a message. He slapped the note into her hand. He cleaned his knife and left the same way he entered.

***

When the team arrived, they met up with the CSPT members and determined that the CSPT would process all the scenes and file the report by the next morning. Angie would not be processing with them after this scene. This would free up the task force to continue to follow incoming leads.

The CSPT briefed them on what they discovered. They moved through the apartment walking on the edges of each walkway so as not to disturb the normal walking path.

"The victim's in the bedroom," the CSPT member said. "Like the others, she's bound with her hands behind her back and her feet tied together. She's wearing exercise shorts, a sports bra, and a sweatband holding her hair up and out of her face. Her shoes and socks where on the floor next to the bed and the closet door is open. It appeared as if the suspect waited in the closet and snuck up on her while she got undressed for a shower."

After being briefed, Brooks asked the victim's boyfriend if he would come with them to the office to give his statement while the CSPT processed the scene. He agreed to follow them.

"Hello officer, my name is Steve Miller," he said at the station.

Brooks scrutinized Steve, and he was visibly shaken. His eyes were puffy and watering, his hands were shaking, his face pale, and his voice cracked.

"How do you know the girl in the apartment?" Brooks asked

"I've been dating Janelle for almost six months," Miller stated.

"Can you tell me about her," Brooks said.

"Her full name is Janelle Phoenix and she's 25 years old. Her birthday is April 15, 1989. Janelle and I had plans to go to dinner at six tonight. I arrived at five to clean up. I found Janelle," he continued.

"When I grabbed her wrist to check her pulse, the heart shaped ring I gave her, was missing. I checked her pulse, and realized she was dead. I immediately called the police and waited outside the apartment. I couldn't see her that way. You know? We were going to celebrate our six-month anniversary over dinner and maybe go dancing."

"Where were you before you found her?" asked Brooks.

"I've been at work since seven this morning and didn't leave work until about ten minutes before I found Janelle," he replied.

"Do you know anyone that would want to hurt Janelle?" Cooper asked.

"She got along with everyone and never complained about anyone bothering her," Miller said.

"What about her family?" asked Brooks.

"She has a sister that she talks to frequently, and calls her mom and dad regularly but I don't know their phone numbers. Janelle always kept her phone in her purse so it should be in the apartment," Miller said.

They asked Miller to fill out a written statement detailing everything he did from the time he entered the apartment to the time he left. Cooper asked for Miller's work number and released him.

The team would wait until the morning for the crime scene report. They spent the last 10 hours on the case and needed a break anyway.

"Can I swing by your house for a drink and to relax on your balcony?" Angie asked Brooks. "My neighbor's newborn baby cries all night and the walls of the condominium are thin."

You're welcome anytime," he replied with a slight grin and she followed him home.

At his house, he offered her a beer and they sat on the deck sipping it while viewing the lights slowly moving across the water.

"It is so therapeutic and relaxing to listen to the silence and look at the scenery," Angie said.

"Have you ever been this involved in a case?" Brooks asked.

"Not on the investigative side of a case but processed some severely damaged bodies in other cases," She said. "This case is not bothering me yet but may come back to haunt me in the future. I always separate my job from my personal life and consider cases my duty and responsibility."

After finishing her drink, she started to get up from the chair saying, "I better get home and try to get a good night's sleep."

"You can stay in my spare room, I don't cry too much at night," he said with a laugh. "The room will be free until my daughter arrives if you want a couple quiet nights of sleep. Don't worry, I have no expectations and I wouldn't offer if we weren't friends. I won't tell anyone, but don't guarantee I won't continue to tease you at the office. I thoroughly enjoyed the panicked expression on your face right before it turned red this morning," he snickered. "I even promise to make coffee for you in the morning to jumpstart the day."

"If I weren't so tired from the past couple weeks of sleep deprivation my defenses would be stronger and I would refuse," she said. "But I'm exhausted and need a quiet night and the view in the morning is a bonus. I'll stay."

When she thought of the view, she meant him in his shorts, standing on the deck in the morning. The scenery would be an added bonus.

"The comment you made at the office was pretty funny," she admitted. "I enjoy a good joke, but you better look out, I will get you back someday. Can I borrow a t-shirt I can l sleep in?" she asked.

He disappeared and returned with a holey old shirt with little holding it together.

"I don't think so," she said.

He pouted his lip but returned with a normal t-shirt.

Angie again woke to the smell of fresh brewed coffee. She tiptoed down the hall in hopes of catching Brooks on the deck in his shorts. She walked towards the kitchen, but stared outside to see if Brooks was on the deck in her favorite attire. She felt disappointed when she didn't see him. She turned to walk where she was headed and ran right into him as he stood in front of her. She was embarrassed but hesitated a moment to feel the heat coming off Brooks' chest.

"Good morning," he said.

She returned the greeting. He stepped out of the way and pointed to the coffee, which she quickly accepted.

They arrived in separate cars at the station, and no one was the wiser. When they were at the coffee pot together, he commented, "I preferred the skimpy old t-shirt you wore this morning."

She scanned around quickly and her face turned red. She gave him the evil eye and vowed, "I will get you back."

As she walked away, Cooper approached to get coffee and asked, "Are you feeling okay. Your face seems red and hot, do you have a fever?"

This increased the heat in her face and she gave Brooks a death stare. Brooks laughed and his partner eyed him quizzically. Brooks left Cooper standing at the coffee pot while he walked away with a smile on his face.

The crime scene reports arrived and were waiting in their inbox. According to the report, Janelle had been killed in the same fashion as the other three victims, except, as the last victim, she had been lying down when the fatal wound was administered. This resulted in the wound being deeper and left a bruise on the victim's back where the handle of the knife hit the skin. This allowed the lab to gauge the depth of the wound fully and determine that the knife in question held a 3.5-inch blade. Based on the pattern of the wound, they determined the blade was single sided for the first 2.75 inches and serrated for the last .75 inches. This was consistent with the other victims. The lab obtained a boot impression from the kitchen floor of the victim. This impression contained the same individual characteristics and wear patterns as the boot impressions from the other scenes.

A deputy coroner arrived in the morgue with the victim's body and CSPT witnessed the autopsy since the task force was unavailable. This victim had been stabbed through the heart like the other victims. Janelle had been cut, forming the letter O in her back, after being stabbed with the fatal blow.

Unique differences appeared this time. The victim sustained a bite mark approximately three inches above her navel. The bite occurred prior to the victim's death and left surface bruising. The bite had been discovered during a body scan under an alternate lights source. The fatal stab wound occurred while she lay helplessly on her stomach. This victim received vaginal tearing that would indicate she had been raped. It appeared the rape occurred prior to her death. Once again, they found an ominous note in the victim's hand. It read, "Now I'm done with number four, and I am still alive. We'll see what happens, when I go for number five." The autopsy report was consistent with the CSPT report.

Cooper made a phone call to the coroner's office to ensure that all the victim's body scans were the same as Janelle's. He assumed they were, but didn't want to take a chance.

"Don't get me wrong, I'm not questioning your standards, but wanted to make sure that the other victims did not suffer from any hidden injuries we didn't know about," Cooper said.

"All the victims went through the same process," he was told. "The other victims did not have any hidden injuries that were not reported."

"OK thanks for the information," he said as he hung up.

He informed the team of the conversation. The team now confirmed they were searching for a suspect with a 3.5-inch knife with a serrated blade towards the handle.

CHAPTER 10

Brooks picked up the phone, "Hey, chief? Can you put out another bulletin to the news media warning woman to be on the lookout for anyone who may be following them?"

"I don't think that is a good idea," the chief replied. "The reputation of the department is at stake.   We don't want people to panic and I don't want to point out to the public that you are failing to solve the case."

"Chief, I get it.   However, the killer has already said he would be committing more murders.   How will it appear if information comes out later and we didn't warn people?"

"You heard my answer, Brooks. Quit second guessing me and get back to work."

Brooks slammed down the phone, getting the attention of the whole team.   He relayed the chief's message to Cooper.

"Why are you surprised?" Cooper asked. "You know the chief's philosophy is to deny everything, admit nothing, demand proof, and make counter accusations."

Brooks shook his head and flexed his muscles. "Idiot," he said, getting the attention of the other officers. Brooks never had a problem with conflict.

When Brooks was a senior in high school, at the age of 17, he intervened when his father tried to hit his mother. By the end of the ugly confrontation, Brooks dominated his dad. In the morning, his father was gone.   Never to be heard from again.   They were notified several years later that he had been killed in an auto accident.   Brooks kept his father's past a secret.   He didn't want anyone feeling sorry for him because of his past.

Cooper put on a smile and spoke, "I got a story for you."

"A company once rewarded officers for using their tire flattening equipment during a pursuit.   They sent a uniform pin out to every officer who ended an incident by using their device.   One of those officers is now the chief.   He was a Patrol Sergeant at the time.   He set himself up ahead of the pursuit to deploy the spikes to flatten the suspect's tires.

Did I ever tell you this one?"

They were all listening.   Phone calls were going unanswered as Cooper spoke.

"When the pursuit approached, the chief tossed the device out into the road after the suspect drove past, and the only tires that were flattened belonged to the pursuing patrol car."

"Did they catch the guy?" asked Brooks.

"Yeah, but that wasn't the end of it."

"Please, go on," said Brooks.

"Someone submitted the incident to the company and received a uniform pin. They put the pin on the chief's uniform while it hung in his locker. The chief was embarrassed."

The crew began to laugh.

"I've never heard that story," Brooks said.

With the room still ringing in laughter, the chief came out of his office. He seemed baffled when the room once again erupted in laughter at the shear confusion on his face.

As they were laughing, Angie received a call on her cell phone.   It was the president of the housing association for the condominium where she lived.

"The neighbors flushing diapers down the toilet caused the drain lines to back up," he said. "Because of the back up a pipe burst that fed six condominiums including yours."

"What do I need to do?" Angie asked.   "

"The water will be off for at least a week due to system repairs," he said. "The water shouldn't cause any damage to your condominium, but you should walk through to examine for herself."

After hearing the news, Brooks offered, "I have a spare room and you're welcome to stay if you want."

Jennifer and Cooper also had spare rooms and Jennifer offered to let Angie stay with her as well.

"I will think about it and get back to you," Angie replied. "For now I have to get to my condominium and get what I need for a week before plumbing and repair trucks block me out."

Jennifer received a call to perform an autopsy and would be gone the rest of the day.   Cooper and Brooks were left to fend for themselves reviewing the case.

Cooper received a phone call from Zoe's mother. "Did you return everything of Zoe's that was being held as evidence?"

"The only things we kept were the clothes she wore and some items from the apartment which didn't belong to her."

"We gave Zoe a charm bracelet that we didn't get back," she said. "It held little charms for each of the sports she played. There's one word on the back of each charm. All together, they read, Love Mom and Dad."

"I'm sorry, but we didn't find anything like that. If we come across the bracelet, we'll return it to you." Cooper said

He relayed the information to Brooks and made a note in the case log for the other team members.

Brooks decided to contact Chandra's family and find out if they received her property or if anything was missing.

Chandra's mother sobbed and said, "I can't find a necklace we gave Chandra on her twenty-first birthday. It's a gold necklace with a locket and inside the locket is a picture of the two of us together. I assumed it had been kept for evidence and not thought twice about it."

She handed the phone to her husband.

"I want ten minutes alone with this guy when you find him," Chandra's father demanded. "Whatever happens in that room, no one should interrupt me."

"Your feelings are understandable and we are doing everything we can to find this maniac," Brooks said.

Cooper contacted the patrol lieutenant and asked, "Has anyone contacted Deltin yet?"

"No one has seen him yet," said the lieutenant. "But the information and a picture of Deltin have been given out at the squad meetings and put in each patrol car. We also contacted other agencies within a 30-mile radius with the information."

It's been a long day. What if we call it and go get a drink?" Brooks asked Cooper.

"Sounds good. Let's call Jennifer and Angie to find out if they want to join us."

A few minutes' later Brooks hung up the phone and shook his head no. "Jennifer is still working on the autopsy report. She's going to be several more hours."

Cooper shrugged. "Let's try Angie."

"I'll meet you in a half hour," she said.

"You think you can handle the two of us on your own?" Cooper asked with a wry smile.

"If you get out of line, I'll kick your asses," She retorted.

Cooper and Brooks laughed.

Over dinner, they told her what they found out about Deltin, and the missing jewelry.

"I guess the killer is keeping a souvenir from each victim," Angie said.

"We will never know for sure about Ashley," Brooks said. "All of her family is dead."

Cooper changed the subject.

"Where do you plan to stay, Angie?"

"I'll find a motel for the week or so. I don't want to inconvenience anyone," she said winking at Brooks.

Cooper's private phone rang and he left the table to answer it.

"I've got some new pajamas. Wanna see them?" Angie asked Brooks.

He smiled, "I will do my best to be a gentleman during your stay."

She sighed. "Too bad, but I'll stay anyway,"

Cooper returned to the table and caught the slack jaw expression on Brooks face.

"What did I miss?" Cooper asked.

Angie laughed, "I told Brooks I can't stay with him because I sleep in the nude."

The men exchanged sly glances.

"That works for me," Cooper said. Everyone laughed and continued their meal.

At Brooks' house, Angie put on a pajama shirt that was worn thin in several places and three sizes too big. She sat on the deck and Brooks joined her.

He commented, "I thought you slept in the nude?"

She blushed.

"You don't have to get dressed for me," he said.

She took his hand, and led him towards the bedroom. "I do sleep nude. But I'm not sleepy yet, are you?"

CHAPTER 11

Angie awoke to the smell of fresh coffee and the sound of her cell phone ringing. Brooks' phone started to ring at the same time.

The two exchanged glances.

"This can't be good," she said.

The calls were from the police station.

"Another body," Brooks said. "A 29-year-old female."

"Yeah, I heard," Angie said. "The wife of a wealthy car dealer. She was found at CenturyLink Stadium."

Brooks nodded. "Home of the Seahawks."

Angie smiled, "They say she was found near the west end zone by the custodian at 5 this morning."

All four members of the task force arrived within ten minutes of each other to examine the scene. The CSPT was also on sight waiting for the okay to start processing. As they reviewed the scene from the stands, they found some obvious inconsistencies. This victim was not as tall as the others were. She seemed as if she were only about 5'1" tall. She was nude and the stab wound did not seem as clean or precise as the other scenes. This victim had a bruised and swollen right eye. Her hands were tied behind her back and her feet tied together. The rope was a yellow parachute cord rather than the burlap type rope from the other scenes.

The methodology in this murder was consistent to the information given to the media, but many details withheld were not present. They feared a copycat murder.

They turned the scene over to the CSPT and asked the custodian to find an office were they could talk. Jennifer decided to follow the CSPT with Brooks while Cooper and Angie interviewed the custodian.

They were shown to an office.

"We can talk in here," Tony Bellatino said.

Cooper thought Tony seemed nervous. Angie wondered if he were in shock.

"Tell us a little about you," said Cooper.

"I am 45 years old and worked at the stadium since it opened,"

Bellatino said. "I work security when the Seahawks are in town. Kinda like you guys."

Cooper and Angie glanced at each other as if to say, "Another want to be cop."

The glance made Bellatino more nervous. "I was the last one to leave the facility last night around midnight."

When neither Angie nor Cooper spoke, Bellatino rambled on.

"The heating system failed. That's why I was here so late. When I came back this morning at 4:30, I started my daily walk through. At about 5:00 I saw the body of the woman. She was lying at the entrance to the stadium inside the locked gates."

Angie and Cooper listened.

Bellatino began to sweat.

"I checked for a pulse and called 911," he said. "I didn't know the woman. I didn't lock or unlock any of the gates this morning. I came in the side door of the stadium. That door is always locked."

Angie began to speak but Cooper shook his head no. Bellatino began to visibly shake.

"I only got half way through morning rounds checking locks before I found her. Did I tell you that? I don't want to leave anything out. I haven't even gotten to the north or east side of the stadium. I guess those gates might be open. I haven't checked."

"Where were you before you returned to work?" Cooper asked.

"I was at home with my wife. She woke up when I got home last night. She woke again at 4 am this morning to get my breakfast before work. Here's the number to contact her. You can ask her if you don't believe me. Am I in trouble?"

"Did you do something wrong?" Cooper deadpanned.

"No. I found her, that's all," Bellatino replied.

"Take us through the morning gate checks, starting with the gates you missed," Cooper asked.

When they approached the southwest gate Bellatino said, "I see a problem."

"What?" Cooper asked.

"The silver lock on the gate." He explained, "The stadium uses only gold colored locks. One master key will open them all."

Angie handed Bellatino some rubber gloves.

"Put those on and give your key a try," Cooper said.

Bellatino did so and said, "The key won't even go in the lock."

Cooper made a phone call to the CSPT and asked that one of their technicians fingerprint and remove the lock for further examination at the lab. The technician responded, fingerprinted the lock, carefully cut the lock off, and placed it in an evidence bag.

"Tony, go ahead and replace the lock when we've completed the rest of the walk around," Cooper said.

No other gates were unlocked or contained a lock that was not authorized. Tony was released, but told to stay away from the victim and the area between where the unusual lock had been found and where the body lay.

Brooks and Jennifer met up with Cooper and Angie. They glanced at the victims ID. It identified her as a 29-year-old born in August of 1986.

"Her name's Diane Walker," Brooks said.

They recognized her from the commercials she acted in with her husband to advertise his car dealership. In the commercials, she usually sat on the hood of a car in a skimpy outfit. Her husband would talk about how hot his deals were while pointing at her, or the car, no one knew for sure. His name was Dallas Walker and he was known as the biggest car dealer in the city.

Brooks investigated the victim, while Cooper spoke with her husband. The ladies would interview friends and family.

Cooper contacted the victim's husband and asked, "Can we meet somewhere and talk?"

"What is this pertaining to?" Dallas asked.

"Your wife," Cooper said.

"I haven't talked to her since breakfast yesterday, is she in trouble? I'm at my car dealership and would be happy to talk to you here," he replied.

Cooper met him at the dealership and told Dallas, "Your wife was found dead this morning."

Dallas smugly scrutinized Cooper and said, "Really, she's dead? You're kidding."

Cooper assured him, "I am not kidding," and noted the unusual response.

In Cooper's experience, each time he informed a loved one that someone had been killed the normal response was to ask questions. The usual questions were "What happened, when, how did this happen, who did this?" When a person did not ask these questions, it was likely they knew the answer because they were involved. This made Cooper suspicious and he asked Dallas to meet him at the task force office to continue the interview. Dallas agreed.

Cooper spent his life being the best at everything he did. In high school, he lettered in four sports with ease. Football was his favorite sport but he also played basketball, baseball, and was one of the fastest in the state in track. His 6 foot 3 frame, good looks and natural athletic ability caught the attention of most the women in high school and college. Cooper received several scholarship offers in multiple sports but decided he wanted to focus on football. Although he enjoyed sports, at the time, he was still in search of his purpose in life. He now lived that purpose.

Once Dallas arrived at the office, Cooper read him his rights.

"I understand my rights. I don't need a lawyer. I have nothing to hide," commented Dallas.

Cooper began, "State you name for the record."

"My legal name is Franklin Dallas Walker. I go by Dallas for the business."

"Where and when did you last see your wife?" asked Cooper.

"About 8 am yesterday morning, at our home," he replied. "The cook made us breakfast, then I went to work. I didn't see her again."

"Where were you last night and this morning?"

"I was at home alone all night. I came to work late this morning because I overslept," he replied.

"Can anyone verify that?" Cooper asked.

"The house staff was off, but we have video surveillance which will show what time I arrived home last night and left this morning."

"I will need the video," Cooper said.

"That won't be a problem," Dallas replied.

As the interview continued, Cooper got the feeling that the man in front of him couldn't care less that his wife was dead. He answered all the questions without emotion and matter of fact, as if he where answering trivia questions.

"How's your marriage?" Cooper asked, noticing an obvious

hesitation in Dallas.

Dallas defensively stated, "I loved my wife and am shocked that she's dead."

Cooper repeated his question.

"We had a good marriage, with problems, like any marriage, but we loved each other."

"Did you ever argue or hit your wife?" Cooper asked.

Dallas reacted emotionally for the first time and stood up, leaned towards Cooper and said, "I would never hit my wife, I loved her!"

Cooper thought this display seemed artificial and fake. He continued, "What would your friends say about the marriage?"

He got even more upset, yelled, and crossed him arms as he sat down, "Her friends would probably lie and say I'm abusive and unfaithful because she filled their heads with false allegations!"

"Are you unfaithful or abusive?"

"No." Dallas said as his head nodded. "I need to get back to work, but will help any way I can. Please update me on the case whenever possible."

Cooper ended the interview with one final question that puzzled Dallas.

"Are you left handed?"

"Yes," he answered while glancing at Cooper quizzically.

In Cooper's experience when a person is punched in the right eye, someone left-handed usually struck them.

After Dallas had been released, Cooper ran a criminal history on him and checked his name in the police computer. He found that Dallas had been arrested three times for domestic violence, but his wife always dropped the charges before going to trial. The computer indicated numerous calls for service at the residence for possible domestic disputes. Many of these calls were reported by the neighbors as a man and woman screaming and noises of things crashing in the residence. Upon arrival, the officers were usually met at the door by the couple, and told that everything was fine. On several occasions, the officers requested permission to enter and verify that everything was OK, and the couple refused. The officers noted that both the husband and wife appeared to be agitated and angry.

Brooks' investigation into Diane produced information that the couple wasn't getting along. She was on the verge of filing divorce papers. He spoke to an attorney whose card was in her purse. He discovered that she had filed for divorce, and planned to tell Dallas the night before being discovered in the stadium.

"She's requesting $15,000,000 which is half of Dallas' net worth," the attorney said. "She's requesting half the worth of the business as well as full ownership of the residence." The attorney continued, "This would equal the $15 million."

Angie and Jennifer located several friends of the couple. They were informed that the couple fought quite often. Her friends witnessed one particular fight during a dinner party where Dallas threatened that if she tried to leave him, he would kill her before he would let her go.

"Diane told us two days ago that she was leaving and had already contacted an attorney to draw up a divorce settlement. Diane said she was going to tell Dallas that she wanted out and that the marriage was over," said one friend. "If Diane followed through she would have informed Dallas yesterday morning."

"I never witnessed Dallas hitting her but she often showed up for lunch meetings with suspicious bruises. She always played it off as being from working in the garden or outside. She would never get dirty, and she had a landscaper so I didn't believe her."

"Dallas came close to hitting us one night. He thought we took Diane out to meet other men. Dallas is paranoid that we were trying to get her to leave him. He didn't like her going anywhere," two friends stated. "We can't prove it, but Dallas killed her."

Brooks received a call from the attorney.

"I received a call from Dallas," said the attorney. "He threatened to sue me for everything I own if I tell anyone that Diane filed for divorce. Dallas said if the police found out about the divorce, or anything else Diane told me, that bad things would happen. I asked him if that was a threat. Dallas told me, it's a big city and sometimes bad things happen." The attorney continued, "I have been doing divorces for a long time and attached a recording device to my incoming lines for conversations like this one. I will drop off a copy of the tape after business hours. Oh, I remembered something else. Diane told me she put some important documents in a safe deposit box at the bank. She gave me a key in case anything happened to her."

"I am going to apply for a warrant for the safe deposit box. Detective Cooper will be at your office within the hour to retrieve the key and your recording," Brooks told him.

Within an hour Brooks and Jennifer were in the judge's office waiting while the judge read the warrant for the safe deposit box. The judge signed the warrant, but told Brooks that he probably didn't need a warrant if the trustee gave them permission to enter the box.

"I'm covering my bases so evidence isn't lost in a court challenge if the case goes to trial," Brooks stated.

As he received the warrant, Cooper and Angie were in-route with the box key to meet them at the bank.

The safe deposit box held an abundance of evidence against Dallas. The box contained dozens of pictures of Diane in various states of dress showing bruises on different parts of her body. On the back of each photo, in Diane's handwriting, was a description of the injury and what implement made the injury, and the date. According to the written comments, Dallas caused all the injuries. Each photo appeared to be a selfie.

Account books were found under the photos in the safe deposit box.

"Dallas has been hiding money from the IRS," said Angie.

"And Diane kept track of his illegal transactions, if these books are accurate," Cooper added.

"We can turn that portion over to the IRS for them to do an investigation," Angie said.

Cooper nodded.

"Here is a list of charity donations that are fraudulent."

Cooper nodded again. "And scan some of these employee names on his payroll, Needa Sellacar, Craven Moolla, and Wanda Sellya. Those can't be real names."

The last item in the box was Diane's will. She signed and notarized the document two months earlier and left all items to be split among ten friends listed in the will. The will clearly indicated that a lawsuit should be filed if anything suspicious happened to her causing her death. The lawsuit was for the items listed in the divorce settlement to be shared among her friends. The team read enough and removed all the contents of the box as evidence.

They returned to the office and contacted an IRS friend of Jennifer's.

They informed him of the evidence they recovered and he was more than willing to investigate further. The photos of Diane's injuries wouldn't be allowed in a domestic abuse case. They would be allowed to establish his character in a trial.

The contents of the safe deposit box immensely increased the case against Dallas, and for that, the team was excited. They were disgusted and saddened, however, by the photos they recovered.

As the team prepared the case against Dallas the news media reported on Diane's murder, and that Dallas is the prime suspect. It appeared that someone on the task force, or one of the crime scene techs, leaked information to the press. Midway through the report, they discovered that Dallas himself called the media and set up a conference in order to get pity and shamelessly plug his business in the background.

He told the reporter, "I have been harassed by the police. They are only investigating me as my wife's murderer, rather than finding the true killer."

He requested the camera pan through his car lot while tearfully stating, "She was always around the lot to help sell cars." He of course mentioned his car dealership several times in the interview.

Jennifer's friend at the IRS called and said, "We are going to serve a warrant on Dallas tomorrow. We froze all his accounts and property until the case is resolved."

The team was elated that Dallas would start to get what he deserved, and they planned to continue investigating Diane's death.

The team felt they focused on the right man for Diane's murder, but questioned if this related to the other murders. They would have their answer in the next 24 hours.

CHAPTER 12

The serial killer task force received a call to respond to the Walker residence at 7:00 am the next morning. They assumed they would be assisting in serving the IRS warrant on Dallas Walker, and be able to retrieve the security footage that he promised to provide. When they arrived, they got more than they bargained for. IRS vehicles weren't at the residence and they spotted what they assumed to be a housekeeper sitting in the back of a patrol car. The CSPT truck was also on the scene. The chief met them outside the front door.

The chief briefed the team and said, "Dallas is dead. The killer stabbed him to death and left him lying at the bottom of the stairs with two videotapes. The tapes are marked surveillance 12-05-14 to 12-07-14. The CSPT already finished the main area of the house."

The team entered the scene and witnessed Dallas at the bottom of the stairs by the living room. He was face down on the tile floor surrounded by blood. His right eye bruised and almost swollen shut. His hands were tied behind his back and his feet tied together with the same type of rope as the first four victims. He sustained multiple stab wounds in his back that shaped the letter E. They spotted a note in his hand but did not want to disturb the scene by removing it. They verified the CSPT took photos of the videotapes and overview photos of the scene before removing anything. Cooper secured the two videos as evidence and told the team they needed to view them. Once at the office he made copies of each video and logged the originals into evidence for the CSPT.

Back in the task force conference room, they began to view the first video. They fast-forwarded to the time when Dallas said he last saw his wife. Since the video activated with motion it started and stopped at different times of day. About 30 minutes into the video, they discerned a difference in how the tape activated and skipped two hours ahead. This was different from the way the motion-activated video recorded each other time. They made note of the time in the video and would request the computer specialists examine the tape for tampering. They continued to view the video until well after the time Diane was discovered at the stadium.

Brooks exchanged the tapes and they began to examine the second video. It appeared to be a copy of the first video. When they reached the time they made note of in the first video, the tape did not skip. It showed Dallas and Diane having an argument. They were at the bottom of the stairs by the living room

"They are having a nasty fight," said Brooks.

"Sure are. He knocked her out with a punch to the right eye," said Cooper.

"He's carrying her outside, What's he thinking?" asked Brooks.

"He put her in the truck. Now he's coming back in the house."

"Cooper, is that a knife he grabbed from the kitchen?"

"Yep, and now he's headed back to the car. He put the knife in the passenger's seat."

"I guess he likes the knife better than his wife," Brooks snickered.

"There he goes," Cooper said. "He's driving out of video range."

The camera became active again at 5:00 a.m.

"And he's back," said Brooks.

"What's all over the front of his shirt?" asked Cooper.

"I'm betting it's her blood."

"I think your right," Cooper said. "He putting his shirt in the fireplace and is letting it burn."

"Let's fast forward to the time of Dallas' death," Brooks said.

They scrutinized the video as a masked man entered the front door of the house. He found Dallas and the detectives witnessed a brief confrontation. The man forced Dallas down stairs and into the living room.

"The guy in the mask is asking questions," Brooks said.

"Uh huh, and Dallas is pointing," Cooper said.

"He's pointing towards the surveillance room," Brooks said. "Now he's tying Dallas to the chair."

"This is a fancy surveillance system. It records sound. Let's hear what they're saying," Cooper said.

Cooper fiddled with the system and they began to hear background noises. Time passed while the two men talked.

"He's leaving Dallas tied to the chair," Brooks said.

"The video followed the masked man right to the surveillance room."

Cooper said.

The team saw the intruder enter the video room and he did not emerge until almost an hour later.

The intruder comes back to Dallas holding two videos and begins to speak. He asks questions about Diane's murder.

"I will do to you what you did to your wife if you lie to me," the intruder tells Dallas.

"I had nothing to do with Diane's death."

The intruder put a set of brass knuckles on his left hand and punches Dallas in the right eye.

"That is what you did to your wife and lied to me about it," the intruder says. "Now do you believe I will do what I said?"

Dallas began to cry and beg for his life.

"Tell me the story of your wife's death." Dallas is informed, "If you leave any details out, you will not live to lie about it again."

"I had an argument with Diane," Dallas confesses. "We fought and I punched her in the face and knocked her unconscious. Diane told me she's divorcing me and taking everything. I swear, I didn't plan to kill her, but she made me so angry. After I knocked her out, she lay on the floor unconscious and I thought I had better end her life or she will take everything I own. I picked her up and took her to the car. I realized at the car that I needed something to kill her with and returned to the house. When I walked into the kitchen, I thought of the idea to stab her and make her death look like the serial killer murdered her. I'm guessing that's you"

"I drove to the stadium thinking that no one would find her for weeks since the football teams out of town," Dallas continued. "I broke the lock off with my tire iron and replaced it with one of my own. I carried Diane into the stadium and put her face down inside the west entrance. I pulled out the kitchen knife and stabbed her in the heart," Dallas relayed. "I hit a bone the first couple of times and finally got the knife to go through. I cut her back until the letter T was cut into her. I thought that would get me off the hook, set up the serial killer, and save me from divorce and bankruptcy."

The intruder listened motionless throughout the story.

"The truth shall set you free," the intruder said.

"Since I told the truth you said you wouldn't kill me."

He cried and pleaded for his life. The intruder placed his hand on his face and rubbed it as if thinking. He turned Dallas toward the camera.

"Is everything you admitted the truth?" he asked Dallas.

"Yes, I swear it is all true."

The intruder knelt down behind Dallas and whispered in his ear.

"Too bad you were so sloppy in copying me."

The intruder made a quick motion behind Dallas' back. Dallas stiffened up, his eyes went wide, his mouth fell open, and blood began to poor from the left side of his chest.

The intruder lifted Dallas off the chair, placing him face down on the floor. He began to plunge a knife in his back repeatedly until he shaped the letter E.

The killer walked away as the pool of blood around Dallas grew larger by the second. He wrote something on a piece of paper and shoved the note into Dallas' hand. He calmly walked out of the residence and into the darkness until the video stopped recording.

The team sat speechless over what they witnessed.

"I don't feel sorry for Dallas, he got off easier than he deserved," said Brooks.

"I am amazed at how calm and calculating this guy is," Cooper said.

"We didn't hear signs of fear or panic in his voice and he methodically and meticulously ended Dallas' life," said Jennifer.

The team all thought the same thing until Brooks said it.

"This is not a killer who began killing one week ago. He's killed before and probably many times."

They all nodded their head in agreement. They were eager to find out what the note said.

"We need to search nationally for a spree killer with a similar mode of operations," Cooper stated.

The team broke up to search the internet. Within an hour, Angie found a similar case in New York City where the suspect stabbed people in a similar way, but did it over a much longer period. The articles indicated that the killer started stabbing woman and cutting letters into them beginning on 1-1-01, 2-2-02, 3-3-03 and so on until the 12th victim died on 12-12-12. The murders only occurred once a year. The killer stabbed the victims in the heart and cut a small letter in the backs of each one. The victims ranged in ages, height, weight, and ethnicity, but they were all woman. After six victims, letters spelled out the words NO MORE. The police thought the killer was done and gone. A month later, the killer left an F on another victim. He continued through five more victims, leaving FOR NOW cut in them. Together they spelled "No more for now." After 12-12-12, the murders stopped and no new leads developed.

Angie contacted the NYPD for a copy of the case file and filled the team in on her findings. She also left a message for the lead detective from the case to contact her ASAP.

"Your killer may be in Seattle and is killing again," she explained in the message.

Jennifer found a similar case in Texas where the victims were stabbed in the back. This killer murdered seven random people within a six-month period of 2012. After further review, the team determined that this was not their killer. The Texas killer was sloppy and disorganized, and didn't cut letters on the victims. He stabbed them repeatedly in a blitz attack before running off. They later found that this killer had been shot by an off duty officer in the commission of a stabbing, leaving him paralyzed from the neck down.

Jennifer found a second case out of Tennessee from 2013. In this case, the suspect killed woman in their twenties from February to September. The suspect would catch them in a secluded area of a park, jogging trail, hiking trail, or other dark areas of the city. He would sneak up behind them and plunge a knife into their backs, piercing their hearts with the first blow. The killer placed them on the ground and cut into their backs. He killed once a month for eight months and disappeared. All of his kills occurred between the first and the fifth of the month and at the end of his killing spree, his letters spelled out M O V I N G O N. The team agreed they needed to investigate this case further.

Jennifer contacted the agency in Tennessee and spoke to the lead detective.

"We doubted the killer would stop on his own," he told her. "After listening to the facts of your case, I know it's the same guy."

"What else can you tell me," Jennifer asked.

"I have vacation coming up and if you haven't solved the case, I would love to come and help out, unofficially of course," he said.

They agreed to talk more when his vacation approached.

Often, detectives are protective of their cases and don't want an outsider finding something they missed, but Cooper and Brooks didn't care how the case was solved. They didn't care about the credit, they cared about the people hurt by this crime. Anyone who might help them end a killing spree was welcome on their team.

Cooper's career in law enforcement started by chance. He registered for a criminal justice class his sophomore year of college to fulfill an elective and discovered his calling. He quit playing football to focus on his career but had to find a way to pay his college tuition for the next two years. During a time when he was desperate for money, a filmmaker approached him. With his looks and athletic ability, he was assured he could easily pay for college with only one or two films a month, as an extra.

In his junior year of college, he began to work for the filmmaker. He appeared in about a dozen films by the end of his senior year. After he obtained his degree, he stopped making films.

Earlier that afternoon the CSPT finished the scene at the stadium as well as the Walker residence later that evening.

Diane's killer had been caught, confessed, and killed in the same day. Even if it was by a serial killer they were hunting. New leads in the case linked the killing sprees to other states. The team hoped that new information would come from the other cases. They thought to investigate other killing sprees somewhere between the end of the Tennessee cases and the beginning of theirs. They would explore this avenue in the morning.

They should have received case files faxed to them and ready for review as well as the crime scene reports from CSPT in the morning. The second crime scene team would not be done with their reports until later.

The team broke for the night. Angie still stayed with Brooks. When they both arrived, they began to discuss the events of the day over a beer.

"I am happy with the way the cases are progressing, but anxious about the new information arriving in the morning," Angie said.

"Let's search the internet for similar cases," Brooks said and headed to his computer.

After only a few minutes Angie exclaimed, "I found one in Colorado. This suspect murdered a woman every three weeks from the first week of

January until the fourth week of July, ten women. The killer refined his targets to woman in their twenties, who were athletic, attractive and active."

They made a note to contact Colorado first thing in the morning and talk to the lead detective to get the case file. They called it a night. They would be back to work in less than seven hours and needed to be sharp.

"Thanks for letting me stay Brooks," Angie said. "And for being discreet."

She stood on her tiptoes, kissed him on the cheek, and disappeared down the hall to her room.

Brooks stood conflicted. Half wanting to follow her to her room to repeat the other night and half-knowing he should let her lead on her own terms. He decided to go to bed and not risk messing up the friendship and partnership they currently enjoyed.

They convened in the morning and Angie told the others about the new case in Colorado.

"I have a connection in Colorado," Cooper said. "I'll make the call."

Cooper briefed his contact and was promised copies within the hour.

"What do I owe you Marshall?" Cooper asked

"I think a 30-year-old bottle of scotch will get the fax machine to work," said Marshall.

"Your scotch will be on its way by the end of the day," Cooper said.

The crime scene report from the stadium provided no new information. The victim had been stabbed in the heart from behind, but it was done poorly. The knife hit a bone several times before going between two ribs and puncturing her heart. Dallas tried to imitate what he saw on the news by cutting a letter in his wife's back.

The lock had been dusted for fingerprints and Dallas left one print on each side of the lock when he grabbed it to push it closed. Diane's body contained carpet fibers that microscopically matched fibers taken from Dallas' trunk. Dallas was left handed and punched Diane in the right eye. Because he punched her with his left hand, a small part of his wedding ring imprinted in her face.

The knife used to kill Diane had been recovered in the trunk of Dallas' car. Dallas' fingerprints were found on the handle of the murder weapon and Diane's blood was on the blade. The confession from Dallas described the details of how Diane had been murdered. Although this confession was coerced, only the killer himself would know some of the details relayed. These details were confirmed by the unedited version of the video. The case would be listed as officially closed.

None of this information surprised them, but the whole team stopped what they were doing to pay attention to the message from the note in Dallas' hand. It read, "I've never killed a man before, now I think I might kill more. He does not count as number 5, but you must work fast to keep her alive."

CHAPTER 13

If the suspect continued with his pattern of killing every other day, He may possibly strike again tomorrow. They began the morning stocking the office with coffee and pre-ordering lunch. Unless he strayed from his pattern and committed another homicide, they would be sequestered in the office for the rest of the day.

Angie finished going over the case file from New York before the others and began to read her notes.

"The suspect has an amateurish way of using the knife for the first couple of victims," Angie said. "It's easy to detect when you view the wounds. The early cuts are rough, the later ones are smooth and made in one stroke. That means the killer is much less hesitant. "

"The killer in this case attacked a wide range of female victims, she continued. "He did not discriminate by any category other than gender. The ages ranged from 20 to 55 and weighed from 105 to 200 pounds. He killed woman of all shapes and sized, races and religions, and financial backgrounds. The crime scene photos in the file showed a progression of sloppy and panicky work in the first couple of homicides, to the efficient killing machine that we are now investigating."

"The lead detective, Mike O'Hara, was the original officer assigned the case. During the investigation, he requested an FBI profiler help give the investigators a better picture of what type of man they sought. This is what the profiler said."

"The profiler's report showed that the killer is probably Caucasian and between the age of 25 and 45," Angie read. "He may be a loaner but has the ability to make female strangers comfortable enough that they don't find him threatening if they were to cross paths. The killer would have been cruel or abusive to animals, and even tortured and killed some as a youth. He would have been a bed wetter into his early teens and gotten into trouble for playing with matches or starting fires. The profiler also felt that the killer would have been sexually or physically abused by his mother and that developed into a deep hatred for woman."

"I think this profile is right on so far," commented Brooks

"The profiler felt that the killer practiced stabbing live or dead animals between kills to get proficient at killing," read Angie "He felt that when the killer is caught, he would be proud of his work. If the interviewer asked the right questions, the killer might confess to gain notoriety, however, he wouldn't confess if he felt the interviewer is of inferior intelligence. He would be threatened by face-to-face interactions with strong male figures, but has no problem challenging those same men over the phone or in writing." The profile concluded by saying, "Based on the way the first victim had been murdered, this would have been the first or second kill."

She called Detective O'Hara in New York and briefly spoke to him. He didn't appear to be too happy that a woman would take over his case. He was a salty old veteran who was used to working with men.

"I don't think a skirt will be able to solve a case that a group of real detectives couldn't," He commented.

She found this offensive but wanted to stay focused on the case. The detective did not have any more information as to who the killer may be.

"If you ever got a suspect in custody," he stated, "DNA evidence is on file waiting to be compared."

"If anyone comes to light, you will be notified right away," she assured him.

She told him about the Tennessee and Colorado cases as well as a short brief on the Seattle case. By the end of the conversation she had somewhat won him over.

"I hope your team is able to solve the case," he said.

She wasn't sure if this was meant to be sarcastic, but thanked him anyway and hung up.

Jennifer pored over the Tennessee case file. She found that the killer progressed from New York.

"According to the reports," Jennifer said. "The stab wounds were smooth and precise. No hesitation marks were evident and the initial wounds were quick and deadly. The killer refined the type of woman he killed and began to narrow the weight and age range of the victims. This time the victims were 110 to 170 pounds and were between the ages of 20-35."

"He still didn't care about ethnicity, race, or financial backgrounds," she continued. "His time performing the homicide is much more efficient

71

and the letters were cut into the victims back as if writing on a piece of paper. He continued the pattern of printing each letter and now the letters were uniform in size. The letters were all capital as before, but they were in the same location on the body almost as if the location of the cuts were measured."

"We have to stop this guy," said Cooper.

This file did not contain an FBI profile, but Jennifer felt that it would still be the same as the other. She also thought that if a profile had been requested, a link could have been made between the two states. She felt that if the cases were compared back then, the killer might not be on the loose now.

The lead detective, Ryan Beechem, called Jennifer.

"We suspected a local butcher," He said, "but he had been out of town for several of the homicides and his DNA didn't match the suspects DNA on file. We dedicated four detectives full time to the case and haven't been able to get anywhere."

She examined the crime scene photos and saw that they were similar to the ones from the local case. She told the detective about the cases in New York and Colorado. He asked that they stay up to date with any evidence from the current investigation. He also promised he would contact them if anything new arose in the Tennessee case.

Cooper spoke to his friend Marshall in Colorado and assured him that he would receive his scotch.

"If the case is solved soon I will deliver your scotch in person and help you drink it too," he said,

"It's a deal."

Cooper found out that the lead detective retired and was no longer in the area. His contact information changed after he retired and relocated. He put Marshal on speakerphone so everyone heard.

"I was the Detective Lieutenant at the time and am familiar with the case," Marshall relayed. "We didn't have an FBI profiler examine the case. The FBI was dealing with a serial killer case on the national level and couldn't spare one."

"Do you know of any information among the department that isn't in the file," Cooper asked.

"All the victims lived alone, but the victims were not all killed at home," Marshall replied. "We found three local sex offenders that we thought would progress to murder but none panned out during the investigation. The same three offenders still lived in the area when the department did their annual sex offender compliance checks last month. The killer did not care if he left DNA. He never left any fingerprints at the scenes. I believe the killer realized his DNA wasn't on file, but his fingerprints may already be in the system," Marshall said.

"I hope we can have that drink soon," Cooper said.

He examined the Colorado case file and saw similarities to the case they were dealing with.

Here's what they had in Colorado," Cooper read. "The killer targeted attractive, athletic, women who obviously took care of themselves. All the victims in the Colorado case file were 20-29 and single. They weren't sure if it was coincidence or important that each victim lived in an apartment. The detective speculated the suspect found young woman attractive and he liked the challenge of having to control someone athletic and in good physical condition. He thought the suspect would be intimidated by powerful men."

This gave Cooper an idea. Cooper understood that the video from the Walker residence would give them an estimate of what this man looked like. He realized from experience that the video surveillance unit would be able to calculate the height and weight of the suspect based off known measurements of other items in the rooms and the exact angle of the camera. He remembered the processing team took numerous measurements of the body and distances from the body to fixed points. It was part of their protocol to take the angle of cameras for this exact purpose. This allowed crime scenes to be re-enacted exactly as they were originally found when the case went to trial, so the jury saw a 3-D image if necessary.

He contacted the surveillance unit.

"Can you guys examine the video to determine how tall this guy is and what he may weigh?" Cooper asked.

"We are already in the process. The CSPT requested it for their reports. We should be done by the end of the day and will fax the information to you when we are finished."

The team took a break for lunch and digested the information along with their food. They talked over the new information. They all agreed the FBI profiler described the suspect accurately, but that the killer was probably 30-45 now. They felt everything else in the profile had been correct, based off their combined experience. Angie told the team about the comment from the old veteran from New York. Cooper and Brooks glanced at each other, smiling.

"Oh, the good old days," they said.

Angie punched Brooks at the same time Jennifer punched Cooper. They all laughed.

"We're filing assault charges for the brutal beating we received," said Brooks.

"China dolls," replied Jennifer.

No one on the team comprehended exactly how tough one of these women had been. After Angie received an ultimatum from her mother, she decided to enlist in the U.S. Marine Corp.

She entered boot camp six weeks later and on the first day thought she made the biggest mistake of her life. Within a month, however, Angie got into the swing of things. Even though boot camp was the hardest thing she would ever do in her life, she survived boot camp. By the end of boot camp, Angie learned she was capable of doing anything she wanted to, not only in the military but also in life. Within six months of completing boot camp, she deployed to Iraq and served nine months during Operation Desert Storm. After her nine-month deployment, she continued to excel in her job. She completed her service and decided she wanted to attend college to stay on her career path. She used her G.I. Bill eligibility to pay for her degree in Forensic Science and graduated with honors. Who knows what would happen if she and Brooks sparred.

As they were finishing their lunches, the fax machine began to sputter again. Cooper retrieved the fax from the surveillance recovery unit.

"Based on the measurements from the scene, the angle of the camera, and the calculations that the surveillance experts completed, they were able to get a physical bio on the killer for us," said Cooper to Brooks. "They calculated that the killer is 5'9" and weighs about 170 pounds. They were able to enhance the video to see green eyes under the mask and make out the general shape of his facial features. This doesn't show his actual face, but did indicate what type of facial shape he has and that he's Caucasian."

"They couldn't get an age but catch sight of the beginning of crow's feet around the killer's eyes," Cooper relayed. "They attempted to reverse the effects of the voice modification he used, but aren't sure if the voice they ended up with is accurate."

The team went over this new information, and all the case files for the next couple of hours. They each took copious notes from the other cases to review later.

They called the CSPT office. They were told that it would take about an hour for the new information to be added to the reports. Someone would copy the report and walk them over to the task force office.

"How many staff worked on the cases today?" Cooper asked.

"11 at the two scenes and they are finishing up."

"Thank them for their hard work," Cooper said. He ordered pizza to be delivered to the CSPT office.

He shared the new information about the killer with the team. They all felt a renewed sense of excitement. They progressed further than any other agency so far and sensed that they would be able to solve the case and stop this psychopath. Cooper ordered dinner for the task force. He understood his team well enough to realize that no one would want to leave until they read over all the files and the newest crime scene reports as soon as they were available.

Dinner arrived before the crime scene report so they reloaded on coffee and sat at the conference room table to eat.

"Someone should keep a hidden stash of whiskey for the poor souls who are forced to work these hours," Angie commented.

Brooks got up as if to get a bottle and they all gazed at him with shock.

"I'm kidding," he said as he sat back down and laughed.

All of a sudden, it became quiet in the room as each member reviewed their notes and ate. About twenty-five minutes later, the office phone rang. It was the CSPT leader making sure someone was still in the office. He relayed they completed the final reports from the Walker residence crime scene.

Since the team saw the video of the crime scene and already received the preliminary information from the surveillance unit, they didn't expect any surprises. After reading the report, several things stood out to them though.

"The killer moved around the house as if he researched where to go,"

Angie said. "He only went into certain rooms of the house, and took a direct path to whatever he wanted. He entered the house and walked directly to Dallas. He walked Dallas to the room where he and Diane fought. The killer's tools were already in place when he tied up Dallas in the living room. He walked directly to the video surveillance room and disappeared long enough to view the video and find the second copy in under an hour."

"I think he's been in the house before," said Brooks.

They reviewed the video footage.

"He is stabbing the letter into Dallas' back rather than cutting it, like the others," commented Brooks. "He must be pissed that Dallas tried to imitate his style."

"The CSPT team is convinced the suspect scouted the house prior to the entry and commission of the homicide. They're going to view video footage from earlier in the day for any new information," Jennifer said. "I can stay and review the video to see if the killer entered the house earlier. You guys go home and rest while I view the videos."

"We will all stay," said Cooper. "We don't need to miss anything."

"The killer wouldn't know to scout the house until after Dallas' TV interview this morning," said Brooks. "That will narrow the search time down to a few hours."

They rewound the video until the time stamp showed it recording an hour after Dallas' interview. Within thirty minutes, they saw someone in dark clothing enter the empty residence with some sort of bag.

"He's going in the house," Angie said. "He's going into the living room with a bag. He's leaving the living room without the bag."

The team realized he didn't carry a bag with him when he left the residence after the homicide.

They immediately contacted the CSPT team.

"We examined the video and our killer went into the house several hours before Dallas got home," Brooks said. "He had a bag when he entered but didn't leave with anything."

"The scene is still secured and can be checked in the morning," said the CSPT leader. "But, since we received pizza, we will send two staff out tonight to search for the bag."

The task force went back to viewing the video.

"He found the video room," said Brooks. "He has two copies of the video before Dallas came home. He had knowledge of what Dallas did before Dallas realized the killer was in the house."

"He's familiarizing himself with the layout of the house," said Jennifer. "He's in the house for less than two hours before leaving the way he entered."

"Dallas didn't come home for a couple hours after that," said Cooper. "This killer must have hidden in the back yard somewhere until he had the opportunity to kill Dallas."

They called the CSPT team and gave them this information as well. Over the next ninety minutes, they reviewed the report.

"We've been here over twelve hours and need to get some sleep," said Brooks.

"Can we come in at ten tomorrow and brainstorm what our next move is?" asked Angie.

"I think we're all spent and ten sounds good to me," said Cooper.

CHAPTER 14

The team slept well that night. In the morning, Jennifer rose first, but still didn't get out of bed until almost nine. She took a shower and put her hair in a ponytail before heading to the office. When she arrived, she saw Angie with wet hair pulled into a ponytail, while Cooper and Brooks threw on hats after showering and not shaving.

Obviously, this case was taking a toll on the team, but the information from yesterday gave them a good feeling about closing the case. They began the day by comparing the suspect information to Marvin Deltin's bio.

"He meets all the known aspects of the FBI profile of the killer, Brooks said. "According to his driver's license, he's 30 years old, 5'9" and weighed 180 pounds, with brown hair and green eyes. These are all within the measurements from the video."

"Deltin's case file indicated he was cruel to animals as a child," said Angie. "He was physically and sexually abused by his mother."

"We need to step up our effort and find this guy," said Cooper.

He was now suspect number one.

They reviewed his work history and found that he couldn't keep a job for long. The longest job that he maintained was as a meat cutter for a little over six months. He also worked as a cook several times. Most of his jobs needed good knife skills. They needed to research where he lived when the other homicides occurred out of state.

They began by contacting the other states. They requested information on anyone with his name and date of birth through the Driver's License Bureaus. Each state returned a list of at least five people with the same name and date of birth. They requested driver's license photos of each person and received them in their email within minutes. They studied all the photos received and none matched Deltin. This meant that Deltin did not acquire a license in that state, but he still may have lived or visited those locations so he couldn't be ruled out.

Jennifer contacted her IRS friend and asked, "What do I need to get copies of Deltin's tax records. I am hoping they indicate where he lived and worked over the last few years."

"I need a warrant to release them to you, but I will answer questions over the phone to rule him out," he said. "It will take two days to get the file through the IRS request process and I'll call you back to discuss the case. I still owe you one after this, but we're almost even now."

"You don't owe me anything," she told him.

The team stared at her with interest after she hung up the phone.

"I'm not going to discuss it now," she said walking away and leaving them wondering.

Cooper checked with the shift lieutenant to find out if anyone contacted Deltin. They couldn't locate him, but were still searching. Cooper gave him an overview of the new information. The lieutenant said he would impress upon his squads how important it is for Deltin to be found.

Angie followed up with the cell phone companies on the administrative warrants and found out that Deltin used a cell phone through a national company. She applied for a search warrant for his cell phone records. They would track the area where he made most of his calls. This may lead to where he works or lives, allowing patrol to focus on a much smaller area.

Angie wrote up a warrant because Deltin is an unregistered sex offender in violation of the law. He failed to register his address, current phone number, work location, work phone number, and according to the PO's report, is at high risk to reoffend. He was also a suspect in multiple homicides and is unable to be located. She requested to be able to access his cell phone records, only in order to try to track him to his work or home. The judge said it was thin but would grant the warrant after the prosecuting attorney gave it a once over. She returned with the warrant, after the prosecutor changed some of the verbiage to suit what the judge wanted.

She took the warrant directly to the cell phone company main office. Within thirty minutes, she acquired his cell phone records for the past six months. A majority of Deltin's calls came from two areas. He also made a few calls between the two locations. She ran a check for all vehicles registered to Deltin. The last vehicle registered to Deltin was a green 1964 Ford Falcon four door. He registered the car less than one month ago and it finally appeared in the computer records this week. She realized the address on the registration was not valid, since they already searched for him at that residence. She made up a flier containing Deltin's information, the vehicle information, the area of the cell phone calls, and why Deltin was wanted. She distributed them in the squad room meeting area and with the shift lieutenant.

"With the new information we should have him in the next couple days," the lieutenant assured her.

"Don't have anyone stop him," Angie said. "Follow him home undetected so we can serve the arrest warrant in his residence.

"Sounds good," he replied. "I'll tell my patrol shifts and let you know when Deltin's located. For the next couple of days I'll also station the 20-person traffic unit in the two areas where Deltin made his phone calls."

At noon, the team was notified of another homicide that matched their killer. The victim was a 22-year-old female name Julie. She had been stabbed in the back and found by a co-worker name Janice who came to check on her because she missed work. They arrived at the scene after the CSPT team. They left the scene to CSPT and took the witness to the office for an interview.

Julie and Janice got out of bed that morning and prepared for the day. Janice was leaving when Julie returned home from a run. Julie sent her mother a text about a guy in the parking lot that made her feel uneasy. She jumped in the shower, knowing she would have a magnificent day. Her office would be celebrating the first hundred pounds that the staff had lost. She began to get dressed when she heard a knock at the door. She answered the door and before it was all the way open someone grabbed her around the throat. Her joy quickly turned to terror. The attacker rushed in and drove her to the living room wall. She fought to get his hand off her throat. She became light headed and struggled to stay conscious, unsuccessfully. When she came to, her hands were tied behind her back. The attacker was wearing a white plastic suit. He sat on her back. She grabbed the attacker's suit in an attempt to get ahold of him. He pushed her head down and forcefully grabbed her wrists, squeezing them. He turned her over and she set eyes on the face of the man from the parking lot.

He gazed at her like a starving man at a steak.

"Please don't hurt me," she pleaded.

"Don't worry honey we're gonna have fun," he said with an evil grin.

She tried to kick him off and twist her body away. He grabbed her by the throat again and choked her unconscious again. This time when she regained consciousness, she realized he removed her pants and underwear, and opened her shirt and bra. He assured her that if she tried to fight again he would kill her. She mentally vacated while he raped and sodomized her.

She no longer ignored him when he bit her twice on the abdomen. She stared at his face and caught a glimpse of satisfaction and joy. He turned her onto her stomach again and climbed off the bed. She assumed he would leave, and then she felt the knife plunge into her back. She felt searing pain for a few moments before feeling a sense of inner peace and calm. She bled out. The killer cut the letter into her back. He made a vertical cut on her left shoulder blade. He made three equal horizontal cuts that joined the top, middle, and bottom of the vertical cut. He removed his suit at the front door and walked out of the apartment undetected.

***

Back in the office, Cooper and Brooks interviewed the witness. Her name was Janice Johnson. She was 25 years old and worked with the victim for the past two years.

"Can you tell us about Julie and her regular habits?" Copper asked.

"My friends name is Julie Michaels," said Janice. "She's only 22 years old. Julie lived in that apartment for six months." Janice tearfully continued, "Julie hadn't had a serious boyfriend in over a year but dated a few men off and on. She didn't want anything serious because she wanted to develop her career before she started settling down and having a family. Julie and I met at work two years ago and immediately hit it off. There were only a few people our age in the office so we were naturally drawn to each other. Julie and I are good friends, and we developed into more than friends."

"What else can you tell us?" asked Cooper.

After a short break to blow her nose and wipe her eyes, Janice went on.

"Even though we are both straight, we experimented with each other and I found it quite comforting to have that type of relationship with someone who understood me as well as Julie did. We agreed that it is a friend with benefits relationship. We were both honestly okay with that. We were able to fulfill our physical needs without all the drama of dealing with an aggressive type guy who is only interested in what's in our pants rather than what's in our heads. We both continued to date other people, but seldom engaged in sex with them."

"Did Julie ever tell you about her life before two years ago?" asked Cooper.

"Julie loved ballet dancing from the time she was six until a year ago when an injury forced her to quit. She felt devastated, but began to enjoy the extra time for other physical activity. Julie is active and rarely wants to sit around. She enjoyed running on the waterfront early in the morning and going for a long walk at the end of the workday. Julie even organized a lunchtime walking group from the office and several people lost weight."

"Do you know anyone who would want to hurt Julie?" asked Cooper.

"I don't know of anyone who would want to hurt Julie. She didn't have enemies because she is so kind and sweet."

"When did you last see Julie," asked Cooper.

"I left Julie's at 7:30 this morning after spending the night. Julie was getting back from her run and hopping into the shower."

"Did you notice anything unusual about this morning?" asked Cooper.

"When I left the apartment I saw a man sitting in a car in the parking lot. I would not normally spot this, but the man wore gloves. He also wore a fake beard and mustache. He seemed out of place and when he saw me staring at him he quickly glanced down and away. I thought about calling the police, but I convinced myself I was being paranoid. Maybe if I called, she would still be alive." She began to sob.

You can't blame yourself," said Cooper. "Can you tell me anything about the man or his car?" asked Cooper.

"He sat in a white older car with rust on the edges of the hood. I don't know cars well so I can't tell you what kind. The man was average sized, not skinny and not fat. What made me suspicious was the light brown hair on his head, but the beard and mustache were jet black. The driving gloves seemed odd too, while he was sitting in the car. I didn't get the license plate and never saw the man before today."

"Please continue," prompted Brooks

"I returned to check on Julie at 10:00am and found her stabbed to death in the bedroom."

"Please try to remember what you did when you returned to the apartment at ten this morning," Cooper said

"The front door was not shut all the way but resting against the door jamb. I opened the door and called for Julie. I saw the picture of the two of us was not by the front door. As I walked down the hall, I spotted blood drops on the carpet coming from the bathroom and began to panic. I stayed to the side of the blood so I wouldn't step in it and ran to the bedroom." She continued, "I saw Julie face down on the bed with blood all over the back of her shirt. I went to her and checked for a pulse but she didn't have one. I saw the cut in Julie's back and a big letter E."

"Are you sure the letter was an E?" asked Brooks.

"Yes," she said.

"Okay, go ahead," Cooper said.

"I realized someone might still be in the apartment and ran for the front door screaming for help. I haven't been back inside," she concluded.

Janice gave Brooks the contact information for Julie's family and received a ride back to work. Cooper called Julie's boss.

"I am sorry to inform you that your employee, Julie Michaels, was killed earlier today," Cooper said. "I need a list of employees she worked with."

"Why do you need an employee list? None of my employees would do this."

"In most cases people are killed by someone they know, a family member, a coworker, a boyfriend, etc.," said Cooper. "We have to investigate everyone. I apologize if that is callous or insensitive, but it has to be done."

"I understand now," said Julie's boss.

"Do you know if Julie had a conflict with anyone in your office?" asked Cooper.

"Julie is a shining star in our office," said her boss. "She has been a real boost to morale and motivator for many staff. I don't think anyone in the office held any ill feelings for her."

"Thank you for the information and we may contact you if we have any more question," Cooper said as he ended the call.

The team began to pick apart Julie's life for similarities with the other girls, while Jennifer contacted Julie's parents. Julie's parents only lived an hour away so she decided to contact them in person. When she arrived at the residence, she was met at the door by two concerned parents. She identified herself and they invited her in.

"Why are you here to talk about Julie?" they asked.

"I am afraid I have some bad news," Jennifer said. "I am sorry to tell you that Julie was killed by an intruder this morning."

Julie's mother collapsed and was caught by her husband. They moved to the living room and set her on the couch to talk.

"What happened? Who did this? Did you catch them?" they asked.

"Someone entered Julie's apartment and stabbed her to death this morning," Jennifer said. "We don't know yet who did this, but that's why I am here. I am hoping that I can get some history on Julie, which may lead to the type of person we may be dealing with. I know this is strange, but we often get information from a person's history that leads the investigation in the right direction. Please take a few minutes and if you are willing, I would like to hear about Julie's upbringing."

With intense sadness they spoke.

"Julie was born on May 10 of 1992 and is 22-years-old, they said. "Julie enjoyed athletics at an early age. We enrolled her in ballet and gymnastics at age six and she excelled. She was an average student but earned straight A's when she applied herself. She was always bored in school. She rarely felt challenged, so she did enough to get by and that's it. Julie lived for recess and being with friends."

"As Julie got older, she wanted to be more and more active," they continued. "In junior high, she wanted to prove that she could do anything a boy could do. I suppose, because she grew up with three older brothers who made her tough. Julie was a tomboy and loved to get dirty, but when the time was right, wanted to be treated like a lady. She tried out for football and was good, but at that time, they didn't allow girls to play, even though she was tougher than the boys were. I am sorry, can we take a break for a few minutes?" they asked.

"Please take all the time you need," Jennifer replied.

After getting something to drink and having time to digest the reality of the situation, they put aside their emotions to help Julie.

"In high school, she began to become a beautiful girl and all the boys wanted to be around her," her father said. "She was interested in boys, but most could not keep up with how active she was. Julie hung out with a lot of different friends, but never sought a serious boyfriend in high school, or even now."

"She is always driven by the next exciting thing," her mother said. "She is an adrenaline junky and can't find a man that is willing to go as far, or fast, as she. Julie wanted someone who challenged her mentally, physically, and emotionally and had not been able to find him yet. She dated several men who were intelligent, but did not want the adrenaline side of Julie. Julie is content being herself, and having a few close friends now. She was too bored in school to go to college and wanted to move to the big city."

"Julie moved to the city almost a year ago, after driving an hour each way for work the previous year," they said. "She has a good friend named Janice. Janice stayed over several nights a week because they used to watch scary movies and neither of them wanted to be alone. Julie told us she was closer to Janice than anyone else. She contemplated asking Janice to move in so she wouldn't have to run home early after every scary movie night."

"We spoke to Julie two nights ago and she sounded as though everything was fine," said her father. "She wasn't worried about anything and told us about getting more people active in her office with a lunch exercise group."

"Wait a minute," said her mother. "I remembered that I received a text from Julie after her run. The text said, "Creepy guy sitting in his car, yikes.""

"What time was that text?" Jennifer asked.

"The phone says I received the text at 7:59 this morning," Her mother said examining her phone.

"Can I take a photo of it and can you forward the text to my phone?" Jennifer said.

"Yes, here it is," her mother said. "If you give me your number I will forward the text right now."

"Thank you," Jennifer said. "You mentioned Julie's brothers, where are they now?"

"Two of them are deployed overseas in the military and the youngest one is a computer programmer living in Minnesota," said Julie's father proudly.

As Jennifer left the residence, she reached into her inside pocket and turned off the recorder she always carried with her. She used her recorder to write her reports later. She formed the habit during autopsies. This ensured that she didn't forget to report anything from the autopsy.

When Jennifer returned to the office, she spent about two hours writing her report and informed the team of what she discovered. It was an abundance of information, but not what they needed to end the homicides.

Julie's body was now ready for autopsy down stairs. Jennifer began the autopsy as she always did. She examined the body with the microscope while the rest of the team looked at the big screen television. Once thoroughly examined, Jennifer began to carefully remove Julie's clothes and the ropes on her hands and feet. These items were placed in a sanitized tray for later exam.

Jennifer examined Julie's body for any unusual marks, etc. Obviously, she sustained a stab wound, but Jennifer searched deeper. This time she went above and beyond, and began to use everything available to her. She used alternate light sources (ALS) and body-imaging equipment on loan from the crime lab for this case. She washed the body, and all draining water collected in a microscopic filter that caught particles or fibers. She would also scrape under the fingernails and examine her teeth to see if Julie bit anything of the killer. The final step before beginning her cuts, Jennifer would have a tent placed over Julie and heat superglue. This creates a gas that adheres to finger oils and allows her to see fingerprints on the body. This rarely produces anything, but all these steps were now part of the case protocol, and would be done with every body in this case.

The super gluing did not produce anything new. Handprints appeared on Julie but no fingerprint ridges. Either the killer wore gloves, or the oils from the print were already absorbed. The ALS showed Julie suffered some bruising under the skin on her wrists that would not be consistent with the rope that tied her. It appeared as if someone with a strong grip grabbed her wrist, and that may have been how he controlled her. She also showed signs of bruising under the skin around her neck. This bruising may have been made by the killer's hand.

The handprint helped the team. Most people will grasp something with their dominant hand. The killer grabbed Julie by the neck with his left hand. The killer was probably left-handed.

Jennifer examined the water filter and found fibers from Julie's clothes as well as carpet fibers. She recovered a microscopic particle of white plastic in the filter that Jennifer couldn't identify without further examination. She found the same plastic under Julie's nails. She ran the plastic through a chemical analysis that breaks the material down into its basic composition. She put that chemical signature into the computer for comparison of known items.

She found that the plastic was the same type used by the CSPT in their crime scene processing suits. Hazmat used these suits for minor cleanup, and other companies for protecting the person or the clothing of the person from harmful chemicals or products. This particular chemical make-up had been used in the suits from 2000 through 2008, when a flaw in the composition occurred and the product was discontinued. Hazmat and Police agencies were no longer allowed to use the product produced in those years.

The rope was examined and compared to the previous scenes. It was a perfect match to all the other homicides in this case. This doesn't seem like much but Jennifer thought of a saying her father used to use. "How do you build a bridge? One piece at a time." The same was true for a case. Each minute piece of evidence helped build the bridge to a suspect and conviction.

The examination of Julie's body would reveal more. The exam indicated the suspect choked her unconscious prior to being tied up. Jennifer found pinpoint sized red spots in her eyes and the inside of her lip, which is a sure sign of lack of oxygen to the brain. This is more commonly known as petechial hemorrhaging. This would be consistent with the marks on Julie's neck. It appeared the killer choked her unconscious with his hands. This allowed the killer time to tie Julie's hands behind her back before she regained consciousness and resisted. Julie had been raped and sodomized but no sperm was present. Jennifer discovered two bite marks. One bite mark was above Julie's navel and a second was below her navel.

Jennifer noted that the abrasions on Julie's wrist were much more severe than on her ankles. This would be consistent with a victim whose hands were tied longer than her feet. Julie obviously struggled against the ropes on her wrists for much longer than her ankles. Her feet were probably not tied until the killer finished raping her. Based on the lack of significant abrasions on her ankles, Julie's feet were tied within minutes of her death.

When Julie was turned over, all four members of the team were stunned. She had the letter E cut into her back identical to the one on Dallas' back except this one was cut in. They assumed she would have a different letter. Did they have another copycat killer? They feared the worst. Jennifer continued her exam and found that the wounds were the same as the other victims. Julie had been stabbed through the heart first. After her death and the blood stopped pumping, the killer cut into her back. Jennifer recognized the same killer struck again and it was not a copycat. They were confused why the letter E was now used twice.

CHAPTER 15

At the completion of the autopsy on Julie Michaels, the team received small tidbits of new information, but nothing case-breaking. They all understood that a break only took one small piece of evidence to change a case, and did not discount anything. They returned to the office to find the CSPT team cleared Julie's apartment and were at the office working on reports and logging evidence.

They ordered lunch and sat in silence as they ate.

All of a sudden Angie cried out, "I've got something," scaring the rest of the team.

Cooper even dropped his sandwich and reached for his duty weapon.

"This better be good, I warned you about scaring me," he said.

"Scan the birthdays of the victims," she said. "The first one killed was born in January, the second in February, the third in March, the fourth in April and not including Dallas, the fifth in May. The suspect's killing by the number of their birth months. The killer somehow knew their birthdays before he killed them. He would have to access records or some kind of information with their birthdays and addresses. This information is protected, and most people don't give it out."

"That might be important," Brooks said. Let's keep that in mind while we investigate each victim."

"Nice work, Angie," said Cooper. "That deserves an at-a-boy, but remember one Aw shit wipes out a thousand at-a-boys."

Angie began going back through each person's history and talk to their families and friends. She needed to find out the link between the victims. Was it a common Doctor, Dentist, Psychologist, or Chiropractor? She was convinced someone accessed the victim's personal information. The killer not only accessed their birthdays, but also their addresses. This link needed to be explored. This was her mission on the team now and she would not fail.

The CSPT report was in and copied for the team. According to the report, the victim had been alone in her apartment when the killer entered. They discovered no signs of forced entry and the killer was no longer leaving his DNA on the victims. He cleaned up his process once again. The killer stabbed the victim the same as the others. He left the letter E again. The differences this time were that he bit the victim, which only occurred in the last case. He raped the victim, which only happened twice before, and he sodomized this victim, which was a first. No boot prints were found this time and the suspect covered his tracks through the apartment.

"He's learning from his mistakes," Brooks said. "But how does he know what his mistakes are when the department didn't release that information."

The report also said there was another hand written note. This note read, "I had not planned to kill a man, it threw me out of whack. By repeating letter E, I am back on track. I'll see you soon, with number six. Better catch me pretty quick."

Angie started filling out search warrants for the victim's mail, bills, and medical records to compare for a common link. Within a couple of days, the team would have more paperwork than they knew what to do with. In that paperwork, they might find the link to catch the killer.

Jennifer completed her autopsy report and headed to her office. Cooper and Brooks planned to interview friends and relatives of the last two victims and would now include questions about doctors, dentists or any other common links.

By the end of the day, the team completed their tasks. Angie compiled four warrants signed by a judge for them to start serving in the morning. Jennifer completed her report and did not find any inconsistencies between her report and CSPT report. Brooks and Cooper spent hours conducting interviews with no new leads.

As Brooks was leaving for the night, he received a call from his daughter Lexi.

"I wanted to make sure you were still up for us to visit dad," Lexi said. "Do you still have room?"

"I will reserve the room," he said excitedly.

"How are you doing with the case?" she asked.

"I am leaving the office and not thinking about the case again until tomorrow," he replied.

"Call me back when you get home dad, and we can talk more," Lexi said.

"Okay give me about 30 minutes," Brooks said.

After arriving home and getting himself a drink, he called Lexi back.

"How are you and your mother doing?" he asked.

"We are fine, but looking forward to a break from school and work," Lexi said. "I finished my junior year early and should be able to graduate next fall. I will start my residency somewhere and the real work will begin.

"That's great," Brooks said.

"I am looking forward to finishing my degree and doing the actual job rather than sitting in a classroom. You'll be my first patient, and I am going to make you change your diet to something healthier, and make you stop drinking."

"Don't you want to go into a different field of work, like being a pizza maker or a brewer, so I won't hate visiting you at work?" he replied.

They both laughed and she made it clear she was going to make him healthy if it killed him.

"Mom has been working a lot of hours to pay for the trip and to get the time off," Lexi said. "She is always tired and complains about the hours, but wants to make the trip."

"I'll pay for whatever she needs and she shouldn't kill herself to make this trip happen," Brooks said.

"Dad, you know how stubborn she is, and that she constantly proves she doesn't need anyone to help her survive."

Brooks remembered some of their arguments because he was trying to help her out and she didn't want or need help.

"I don't talk to you for you to solve my problems," Janet would say. "I talk to you so you can listen and I can vent. Stop trying to be the hero and listen."

He never understood why she got mad at him for trying to help. Apparently, she never understood why he tried to save her when she vented to him.

Brooks and Lexi were still talking on the phone when Angie walked into the house.

"Honey I'm home," she jokingly said.

This set off a myriad of questions from Lexi.

"It's my partner being funny," Brooks explained.

She was not convinced, but let the questions go unanswered.

"It would be nice to know that you have someone to take care of you," she said.

"I don't have time for that," he replied.

"You need to make time," Lexi said.

"Hey I'm the parent here," he said laughing.

"Someday your job will be gone and it would be nice to have someone around to share the free time with," Lexi replied.

"It's too complicated," Brooks said.

Lexi sighed.

"Do you have a boyfriend," Brooks asked

"I don't have time right now," she said.

"Hmmm, I think I've heard that somewhere,"

They laughed. She signed off and handed the phone to her mother. Janet got on the phone.

"Who was Lexi talking about being in your house?" Janet asked.

"My partner is here to go over the case," Brooks said. "How are you doing? Lexi is afraid you are working too much for this trip."

"I'm fine and will make it as always," Janet said.

"Can I help?" Brooks asked.

"You're helping enough by letting us stay with you."

"I wish we got together more often," he said.

"It's nice that we can still be friends," Janet said.

"I still regret putting my work first," he said.

"You still do," she replied.

"What do you want to do while you're here?" Brooks asked.

"We want to ride a ferryboat and go to the top of the space needle," she replied.

"The Seahawks will be in town, and if they win the next two games they will be in the playoffs and have the home field advantage," Brooks said. "Do you want to go to a game?"

"I was never fond of football, but it would be fun to go to a game together anyway. I miss you and look forward to some time together," Janet said.

"Me too," Brooks replied.

After going over some travel arrangements, they ended the conversation and hung up.

Angie caught the expression on Brooks' face after she made her comment, so she grabbed a drink and headed out on the deck. Brooks came out a few minutes later. She stared at him as if she was in trouble. He laughed at her.

"You seem like you're guilty of something," Brooks said.

"I didn't know you were on the phone when I came in," she said sheepishly.

"It's fine, but you created a flurry of questions from my daughter," Brooks said. "My daughter doesn't like me being alone. She always wants me to find someone take care of me."

"I agree with her," Angie said.

"Why do woman always want a man to find someone to take care of him," Brooks said. "Can't a man take care of himself?"

"Life can get lonely when you're your own best friend," Angie said. "What do you plan to do when you're not spending ten hours a day on the job?"

"I'll sit on the deck and drink beer," Brooks said. "They'll probably find me dead someday, right in my favorite chair with a half-full beer in my hand."

"That's not funny," Angie said. "I feel sad for you. You need to find a good woman who has the same dedication and drive for her work as you do."

"Do you know anyone," Brooks said as he glanced at her.

She blushed and quickly headed inside.

"Do you need anything, dear?" she asked with a smile.

Jennifer was at the office going over her autopsy report again and comparing the current victim to all the others she worked on. She made note of what she found. Each victim suffered stab wounds through the heart with the first blow and subsequent cuts were administered after the victims were dead. All the stab wounds and cuts were precise and accurate in location and placement. The victim's hands and feet were tied sometime during the attack. Each victim had been killed and left with little evidence. The victims were all of similar age, shape, height, and weight. The first couple of victims removed DNA evidence from the suspect by scratching him and now the killer was wearing protective gear. The first few victims fought their attacker, and the last two seemed to have been subdued quickly. The first victims were not sexually assaulted, but the killer was adding a new act to each victim. Originally, he only killed. He progressed from killing and rape, to killing raping and biting. The last victim had been killed, raped, bitten, and sodomized. She feared he was going to continue to get more violent while the girls were alive. She didn't know how far he would go. She made a brief list of the progressions for the team.

Cooper called Brooks.

"I'm gonna stop by for a beer," Cooper said.

"Okay, but I'm almost out," Brooks said.

"I brought a six pack in the car with me," Cooper replied.

"Cooper's on his way here," Brooks told Angie. "Do you want to leave before he gets here?"

"I'll tell him we were discussing the case," Angie said. "But only if he asks."

"Sounds good," Brooks said.

Cooper arrived before she had time to leave anyway.

"Whose car is that outside?" Cooper asked. "Oh, Hi Angie."

He eyed Brooks and gave him a quick raise of his eyebrow and a wink.

"Shut up!" Brooks said. "She's here discussing the case."

They all sat on the deck commenting about the fortunate boat owners cruising by without a care in the world.

"Most of those people are oblivious to what kind of things go on in their world," Cooper said. "Unfortunately, we've experienced more than we ever wanted too and can't ignore what we know."

The three briefly talked about the case. Brooks changed the conversation.

"Janet and Lexi are coming to visit over Christmas break," Brooks said.

"That'll be nice," Angie said pretending to hear for the first time.

"Good for you," Cooper said. "Enjoy the time while you can."

Brooks went inside to get a drink.

"What's their relationship like Cooper," asked Angie.

"I knew Brooks when he was still married to Janet," Cooper said. "Brooks almost completely fell apart when Janet left him and moved away with Lexi. Brooks almost quit the department to be near them, but decided he needed to let Janet have some room."

"That must have been a terrible time," Angie said.

"He was a mess for a while, but he didn't want to jeopardize a relationship with Lexi later on," Cooper said. "Janet never tried to keep them apart, but the distance prevented him from visiting her more than once or twice a year. Brooks and Janet grew closer after they separated for a while. His relationship with Lexi blossomed, and Janet never said anything bad about him to her."

"Sounds like they put their daughter first," Angie said.

"Yes, they did," said Cooper. "Janet always told Lexi what a terrific man and hero her dad was for saving all those people that everyone else forgot. Those he couldn't save, he would at least get justice for most of them, she used to say. I heard Janet tell Lexi that her dad's partner once described him as a pit bull on crack when he sank his teeth into a case. He would not let go until every scrap of the case lost momentum and was no longer viable."

"He's still the same way," Angie said. "Are they still close?"

"Janet and Brooks will always love each other," Cooper said. "But Janet knows they can't be together because the job is always first."

"What are you guys talking about," asked Brooks when he returned.

"Nothing," said Cooper.

After a few drinks, Cooper got up to go to the bathroom. On his way, he walked by the spare room and caught sight of woman's clothes on the bed and hanging in the open closet. This meant one of two things. Either Brooks began to cross dress in what little free time he had, or Angie was staying with him. He assumed since Angie's condominium was out of commission the answer was the latter of the two. He thought to himself, "You lucky dog, you." He returned from the bathroom and never said a word, at least not while Angie was in earshot.

When Angie went to the bathroom, Cooper jumped at the chance for the scoop. He gave Brooks a barrage of questions about Angie.

"Is she staying with you?" asked Cooper.

"Yes," answered Brooks.

"Are you guys sleeping together?" Cooper asked. "Oh I bet she looks fantastic naked, doesn't she?"

"She needed a place to stay," Brooks calmly replied.

"It doesn't matter what I tell you," Brooks said. "I know you only think about sex when you're not working. You'll assume we're having sex no matter what I say so I won't say anymore. I'll leave it up to your imagination."

Several times, Cooper's assumptions got him in hot water at the office. He received discipline for making a statement about a female officer to the squad room. He quickly learned to shut his mouth and keep his fantasies in his head.

Angie returned and the men both stopped talking at the same time.

She asked, "Why are you so quiet?"

They didn't reply.

"Were you talking about me?" she asked.

"No," they both said.

"Well, at least if you were talking about me, you were having an intelligent conversation," Angie said.

They laughed.

"I better get going," said Cooper after another beer. "I need to get home and get some shuteye before tomorrow."

"I should get going soon too," Angie said and slowly pretended to get ready to leave. "I need to use the bathroom one more time before I go."

This gave Cooper time to leave and she was able to settle back into her new favorite chair.

"The next time we're out here you have to tell a little about yourself, rather than me spilling my guts," Brooks said.

Angie recalled when she received the job offer at the PD. After a year of submitting applications, Seattle PD hired Angie as an evidence technician and forensic scientist. She was afforded opportunities to work at the state crime lab but chose to stay with the police department. Angie wanted to work on local cases in the community she loved.

Brooks never told Angie what Cooper saw and asked about. He wanted her focused on the case and was grateful Cooper wouldn't say anything.

CHAPTER 16

In the morning, the team received the report from the CSPT office regarding what they discovered in Dallas' house. They located the bag the killer left behind and found his hiding spot in the bushes.

The bag contained rope matching that from the victims, duct tape, a set of lock picks, a box of medium rubber gloves, and a folding knife with a 3.5-inch blade. The blade was a standard single edged blade that turned into a serrated edge for the last .75 inch. This would be consistent with the same type of blade used on the victims. The knife was sent to the lab for analysis and did not contain any blood.

They were currently comparing the wound tracks of the victims with a sample wound made by this knife. The knife was not a generic knife but was made by a local knife maker and sold in dozens of knife stores. The knife maker had been contacted and said that he made over three hundred of the knives over the past five years and did not sell directly to individuals.

The hiding spot in the bushes also produced some evidence. Boot impressions were recovered in the soft soil of the landscaping. These impressions matched the ones from the previous scenes. This set had characteristics in the dirt that are more individual from the walking pattern of the wearer. A plaster mold was made of the impression and would be available in evidence should a suspect be found.

They recovered several candy wrappers and a banana peel. All of these items were dusted for fingerprints. It appeared the killer kept his gloves on while he ate. The team recovered a piece of cloth from the shrubbery that snagged while the killer moved in or out of the bushes. This material had been analyzed and was from an expensive type of all-weather jacket. The jacket was manufactured by All Weather Protectants and was only manufactured in 2013. The jacket retailed for $500.00 each. This particular jacket was only sold in the Elite Sports Shop near the football stadium.

Angie made a note to write a warrant for the Elite Sports Shop records of everyone buying this jacket. She realized that if the suspect paid cash for the jacket the warrant would not help, but if a credit card was used the record would still be on file with the purchaser's name.

Jennifer discussed the observations she made in comparing the victims files last night. They thanked her for the update and agreed that these meetings were crucial to make sure every member has all the information. They agreed to have the meetings at least every Monday morning to update the team of any new information or theories.

After the review, the team discussed what type of person they thought they were dealing with.

"I agree with the FBI profile," Brooks said.

"With the sexual activity in the last few murders, I think our killer probably started as a rapist or peeping Tom," Cooper said. "He has obviously perfected breaking and entering without being detected."

"Maybe he isn't breaking in at all," said Angie. "Maybe he is knocking or entering in unlocked apartments."

"As he gets away with more he will get bolder and bolder," said Brooks. "He is obviously brazen enough to do whatever he wants now. He's taunting us."

"He probably got such a rush from raping the victims, that he eventually starting killing them," Cooper said. "He wanted to increase that rush even more."

"That's assuming he raped at all," Brooks said. "Now that he's proficient at killing he's added a new thrill back in by going back to his roots. He's putting his own total package of mayhem together. He's sexually assaulting and raping the victims, marking his territory by biting them, and finishing his quest by killing them and leaving his calling card."

"And yet he somehow escapes undetected," Jennifer said.

"Of course, this is a theory, but based off our almost 85 years of combined experience," Brooks said. "He's probably rather plain and unassuming looking. He's someone that no one would give a second glance to or find threatening in any way. He may even seem feminine and harmless to woman he meets."

"Kinda like you Brooks, you're feminine and unthreatening," Cooper said jokingly. He appreciated Brooks was the best partner he ever had. He also understood Brooks' drive and determination in the job.

At 21, Brooks submitted an application with the Seattle Police

Department and was accepted. Brooks made it clear right away, he was no average employee. He studied Washington Law and comprehended it inside out. Once he was hired, he attended the academy and graduated number one in his class. He wanted to be the best at what he did and would not accept second place. Together he and Cooper were an unstoppable team. If they did not solve this case, it was not solvable.

"What else do you think?" Angie asked.

"He's an average person, with average appearance," Brooks said. "He's good at what he does and probably intelligent because he has gotten away with killing for this long."

All this information, combined with what they already learned from the file and the video, led to a good description of a suspect.

"Deltin's pretty creepy looking," Angie said.

"Yes, but as a sexual predator, he's learned how to be charming and sweet talk people," Cooper said. "I'm sure he can blend in when he wants to. He's still number one on the list, but we won't stop searching for anyone else who fits the profile. We can't afford to get tunnel vision and miss an otherwise obvious suspect."

CHAPTER 17

The Shooting Response Team called the office and said they needed to meet with Cooper and Brooks for a review of the investigation into their fatal shooting of Jonathon Malcom.

"Report to the SRT office immediately," they were told.

The investigators started the meeting.

"The family of the suspect is suing you two for wrongful death," said the investigator. "The department attorneys declined to be involved in defending you. The department doesn't want to appear partial to officers over the public. They don't want the impression that the department not only condoned the use of lethal force, but also defended use of force with department attorneys and resources."

"This is bullshit," Cooper said. "An officer does his job according to all the policies and procedures and is hung out to dry. Next time we'll tell the victim that we would have acted, but the department does not condone officers defending victims of crime if it might result in litigation. Can I get your business card to give to the next victim?"

"You're lucky you weren't disciplined for your actions or terminated," the investigator said. "We decided to give you the benefit of the doubt in a stressful situation."

"What grounds do you have to terminate or even discipline us," Brooks asked.

"It's not important," the investigator said. "My team spoke to about 23 witnesses and several of them did not hear you identify yourselves as an officer. These individuals thought you two shot the other man in some sort of gang war. These particular witnesses saw two men with guns chasing one man and the single man finally stopped to protect himself and was shot by the two aggressors of the confrontation."

"Do we need union representation and an attorney for the rest of this meeting?"

"No," said the investigator.

"We will need copies of all documents that support your findings," Cooper said. "Under union regulations I have the right to these documents since we are being disciplined by not being supported by the department."

"I disagree," the investigator said. "I'm not giving you the paperwork."

Brooks sent a text while they were talking and a union rep knocked at the door of the office within two minutes.

The representative entered the meeting and was caught up on what Cooper and Brooks were told. He immediately made a verbal and written request for the documents that lead to the outcome of the investigation. The investigator understood he had no right to deny the union the ability to defend an employee, so he produced the documents.

Cooper, Brooks and Tim, the union rep, held a private meeting to go over the documents. They agreed to meet back with the investigators when they completed the meeting.

They examined the paperwork.

"Twenty of the witnesses saw and heard us identify ourselves as police and tell the suspect to drop the weapon," Brooks said. "They even heard us tell him to get on the ground while we were in pursuit. Six of the witnesses even testified that the suspect stopped, turned towards us, and began to raise his weapon as if to fire. They continued to say we fired in self-defense of ourselves, and the citizens on the street. Several of the witnesses said we should receive a commendation for our actions in preventing a violent crime in progress."

For some reason all those statements were ignored and the three statements contradicting those were the only ones the investigator focused on," Tim said. "This is no surprise. With the recent budget cuts, the administration has implemented a policy to automatically deny extraneous costs unless the officers involved contest it. You know guys only make the SRT team if they're a yes man that's able to give an outcome to be determined by the chief."

"Don't worry," Tim said. "The union will be filing a grievance by morning requesting that the department provide an attorney for you. The grievance will be filed on the grounds that most of the witness statements supported you, and your actions were within normal policy and procedure set down by the chief himself."

The three men came back into the SRT office and met with the investigator. They laid out the requirements that needed to be met in order to prevent a grievance and further legal action. The investigator was visibly angry about how the situation turned. He understood he was entirely wrong but the chief said to convince Brooks and Cooper to take the original deal or he would not be in the SRT unit for long.

"I can't make that deal without the permission of the chief," the investigator said. "I don't have the authorization to change the chief's decision without his signature."

"This needs to be done today," Tim said. "Or a grievance will be filed in the morning."

As they were leaving the office, they were also given the allegations from the family on the wrongful death lawsuit. The family alleged that their son walked in the restaurant to inquire about a job. When he left, two unknown men began to chase him through the streets until their son stopped to defend himself. The two thugs shot and killed him.

Brooks and Cooper went back to work. Tim was handling the shooting case from now on.

Later that day, Tim made copies of the witness statements and took them to the local union attorney. The attorney spoke to the family. At the end of that call, documents were drawn up stating that based on the witness statements and totality of the information received, the officers and the department would not be paying a settlement in this case. The attorney letter went on to say that if the family chose to pursue this frivolous law suit, the family would be countersued for reimbursement of department and officer's attorney fees as well as mental stress, time loss, counseling and any other costs to the department and officers that resulted from the incident.

Tim and the attorney met the SRT investigator in the chief's office the next morning.The chief was presented with the information of the case as well as the attorney letter to the deceased's family. He was also given a copy of the grievance that would be filed if the chief did not follow department protocol to accept responsibility for officer attorney fees that resulted from the proper performance of their duties.

"After reviewing the information," the chief said glaring at his investigator, "We've made an error. The department will pay the attorney fees. You can send the attorney letter to the family of the deceased suspect to put an end to the frivolous lawsuit."

"Thank you for hearing us out chief," Tim said. "Can you have the letter delivered by the SRT investigator today to end this case, since that is who the family has been contacting.

The chief handed the paperwork to the investigator.

"Deliver that in person by the end of business today," commanded the chief.

"I'll have it delivered today sir," the investigator said.

"The letter will be delivered by you before the end of business, today," the chief ordered. "If the family chooses to sign, it should be delivered back to the department today and these officers will be notified of the outcome before they go home."

The chief was clearly pissed off at the investigator, but couldn't stop the union's request or their attorney letter. Tim and the attorney left the chief's office thinking that they would have a resolution within the next couple of days.

"That's how the incident should have been handled in the first place," Tim said.

Cooper saw the investigator leave the building as he received a text on his phone regarding the chief's opinion. He glared out the window and said, "Dumbass!" He told Brooks and they went back to work.

The team received a call from a local mechanic shop.

"I saw a report on the news seeking information on Ashley Long's car," the shop owner said. "I called to tell you that her car stayed in my shop for the past week. I'm waiting for a special ordered part to come in so I can finish repairs on the vehicle. What should I do with the vehicle, or are the police coming to get it?"

Since Ashley had not been killed in the car and the team now realized it was not in the hands of the killer, they cancelled the BOLO.

"Hold the car for now," Brooks said. "If a family member doesn't call to claim the vehicle in 60 days, the vehicle can be sold to pay for expenses you've incurred."

The vehicle was no longer going to be useful to them.

Angie received the phone records, bills and other documents for the first five victims. With each victim going forward she would file a warrant from the original template and would be able to get the signed warrants served much faster. The team sat down with each victim's paperwork to investigate for numbers in common on the phones, any bills in common that would indicate a link, or anything else in the paperwork to help the case.

After hours of scouring the documents, they discovered that each victim's phone received several blocked calls within an hour of being killed.

"Is it possible that the victims received a call from the killer to verify they were home?" Angie asked. "Does he have their numbers and addresses?"

They asked these questions before, but it appeared they might have their answer. If he called the victim to verify they were home, how did he get them to let him in? No signs of forced entry, tampering with the locks, or windows were found.

"Maybe he was let in?" Brooks asked.

"What would lead these women to believe he was safe to let in?" Cooper asked.

The next victim was discovered and would not provide them any more information. Brooks and Angie responded to the scene and discovered a 27-year-old grade school teacher named Sheina. Her boss, Donovan Stricker, found her. He was pale as a ghost, not thinking clearly, and kept repeating himself. He was obviously struggling with what he witnessed. Stricker agreed to be interviewed in his office.

Sheina showered and prepared for a long day of teaching that morning. She was eating breakfast when someone knocked on the door. She opened the door and let the man in after a brief conversation. As she spoke to the man, she found it odd that he put on a white suit.

"Oh the suit is for your protection," he said. "I don't want to contaminate your apartment while I search for what I explained to you."

She turned to show the man to the other room. Before she comprehended what happened, the man had her arms pulled behind her back and trapped. She glanced over her shoulder in a panic.

"What are you doing," She exclaimed. "Let me go right now."

"I'm afraid I can't do that," he replied.

"Why not?" she asked.

"You realize, I'm not here for what we talked about?" he said. "I'm here for you sweet heart. I've been gawking at you for a couple of days and couldn't wait to meet."

"Let me go and get out you freak," Sheina yelled.

He ignored her comment, picked her up and carried her by the arms to the bedroom. He tied her hands behind her back.

"Please stop, my boyfriend will be home any minute," Sheina said.

"Your boyfriend is already at work and will not interrupt us," he said.

He sexually assaulted her and bit her several times. She tried to scream but he put his hand over her mouth. When the assault was over, he walked her back to the living room before tying her feet

"I don't want you to wait too long to be found," he said. "So I will leave you here in the living room by the window."

She felt a sense of relief. He implied that he was going to leave her alive, but tied up.

"Stand up for me," he said.

She stood and assumed he would soon leave. She suddenly felt the knife forcefully penetrate her back, piercing her heart. She remained alive long enough to feel her blood gushing out of the wound in her back. She smelled a sickening odor. She collapsed to the floor as her life left her. The killer made a vertical cut on her shoulder blade. He made two diagonal cuts. He cleaned his knife, opened the front curtain slightly and left the apartment.

***

"Tell me what you can about your coworker, Mr. Stricker," Brooks said.

"Her name is Sheina Boston," Stricker said. "I drove to Sheina's apartment to see if she was okay. Before that, several of her friends and I made calls to her house with no reply. Since Sheina rarely missed work and always called the school if she was not going to be in, I grew concerned. She never missed work without notification. When I arrived I spotted her through the front window of the apartment. She was surrounded by blood and I called the police. I don't know her birth date but she's 27. I've worked with Sheina for the past three years, but promoted and became her supervisor 16 months ago."

"Why did you go to her apartment to check on her?" Angie asked.

"We implemented a policy to verify the status of an employee. If we can't reach the employee by phone an administrator goes to the employees address."

"Most employers wouldn't go to someone's house if they didn't come in to work," Brooks said.

"The policy came about two years ago after a teacher suffered domestic abuse and was left for dead by her abuser," Stricker said. "If the school implemented the policy back then the victim would have received the medical treatment needed to save her life. As it was, the victim ended up bleeding to death before being discovered and the suspect fled 11 hours earlier."

"Who do you know that may want to hurt Sheina?" Angie asked.

"I don't know of anyone who would do this," Stricker said. "She is dating another teacher and he may have a better idea. His name is Andy Foxx, but I don't think he knows what happened yet."

The team asked to have Andy come to the office and Stricker made a call.

"Andy's on the way," Stricker said.

Brooks took the lead in this interview. He read Foxx his rights and asked if he understood.

"I understand my rights, but don't understand why you're reading them to me," Foxx said.

"Are you dating Sheina Boston?" Brooks asked.

"Yes, why?" Foxx asked.

"I am afraid she was killed," Brooks said.

"What happened, where is she, who did this?" Foxx immediately asked.

"She was killed in her apartment and we need to ask you some hard questions," Brooks said.

Andy was speechless and began to sob. His face turned pale and tears began to stream down his cheeks. He lifted his head to speak but his voice caught in his throat.

"I can't believe it," Foxx said. "Is this real?"

"I'm afraid it is," Brooks said.

"I'll do anything I can to help," Foxx said through tears and obvious confusion.

"When did you see Sheina last?" asked Brooks.

"I spoke with her over dinner last night and we left the restaurant at around 8:30 p.m."

"Where did you go after that?" Brooks asked.

"I went home and as far as I know, she drove to her apartment. I went to work at the school this morning and didn't know anything was wrong until Stricker asked for Sheina's phone number and said she didn't come to work. I tried her phone several times to no avail."

"Did you stay home all night," Brooks asked.

"Yes, I was home all night. I got up this morning and came to work. That's when Stricker asked me for Sheina's number. I've been in the classroom teaching my students until you called me down here.

"Do you know anyone she didn't get along with or had a problem with?" Brooks asked.

"I don't know anyone who would want to hurt her," Foxx said.

"Can anyone verify you were home last night? asked Brooks

"I live alone and was alone all night last night."

Foxx was released backed to work.

Angie requested a criminal history on Stricker and Foxx. Since teachers have to be fingerprinted and a criminal history report done every few years, she didn't expect to get much. It turned out that neither man had ever been arrested, but Foxx was a little bit of a speed demon. He compiled four speeding tickets, but it's a long leap from speeding to multiple murders. Neither man ever lived in the other states where the murders occurred.

CSPT finished the scene and returned to the office. Cooper and Jennifer continued to scour the paperwork from the victims and found no other links. They examined bills, phone records, bank records, searched for common modes of transportation, common interests, and any other avenues. They went so far as to check for parking tickets, court appearances, or lawsuits. They found nothing new.

CHAPTER 18

The team was told that Sheina was in the coroner's office. They all headed down the elevator to Jennifer's lab for autopsy. Sheina's ID indicated she was born in June and was 27. Jennifer followed the same procedures for the microscopic exam, body washing, and clothing removal. When she began to examine Sheina's body, she found signs of rape, sodomy and bite marks. This time the suspect bit her above and below the navel as before but also below her left breast. The bite marks were much harder and did not only bruise the skin. This time the killer bit her hard enough to leave red marks without breaking the skin. She had been tied with her hands behind her back and her feet tied together. Her hands were tied longer than her feet. When she was stabbed, the puncture penetrated her heart and blood began to run down her back, indicating she was standing. The rest of the wounds were administered while she was lying down. The cut wound formed the letter Y in her back in the same precise manner and location as the others. Sheina's hands were examined for evidence and nothing was found under her nails. A note was removed from her right hand. The note read, "Now I'm up to number six, and she is on to heaven. It won't be long, I'm getting bored, and it's on to number seven."

The team was done with the autopsy. They thought about going to the office to read the CSPT report, but decided to review the case with a fresh well-rested mind.

"This case is wearing us down and I'm afraid we'll miss a crucial piece of evidence if we don't give the case a clear focus," Brooks said.

The four headed to the local cop bar called The Padded Cell to have a drink.

"We won't talk about the case until tomorrow," Jennifer said.

The rest of the team agreed.

"Are you still wondering why the IRS agent owed me a favor," Jennifer asked.

"What did you do for him?" Cooper asked.

"I was in my second year as a coroner. I received the body of a young female suicide victim. As I processed this young woman, I found a small puncture mark inside her lip. I requested an in-depth toxicology screen for drugs. During this screening, a drug that would not normally have been found was discovered. It was a drug commonly used to incapacitate a person. Since this drug was in her system, she wasn't capable of shooting herself as was being alleged. She had been murdered. A neighbor was later convicted of killing this young woman. The neighbor was a pharmacist who had access to any drug he needed.

"Oh, my gosh," Angie said.

"He apparently confessed to being infatuated with her," Jennifer said. "She spurned his advances and he hatched a plan to kill her. That young woman turned out to be the agent's sister."

In the morning, they were met with bad news. They received a message to call dispatch first thing this morning. Another body turned up overnight. This was out of character for the killer to strike two days in a row. The team was briefed.

"An anonymous call came in from a phone in an area of the city known for its drug culture," the dispatcher said. "The caller said that a female was located in an alley two blocks west of the giant Ferris wheel that overlooked the Puget Sound."

What time was that?" asked Brooks.

"An officer responded to the area at two this morning and discovered another female victim," the dispatcher said. "We called you because of the familiar stab wound to the victim.

The team read the officers report and found that he discovered the body a little after 2:00 a.m. He approached the body and spotted a stab wound in her back. He also saw that the victim's hand was lying at an odd angle and was obviously broken. He checked for a pulse but did not find one and secured the scene.

The CSPT arrived at the scene around 3:00 a.m. and they were almost done with their processing. The body was on its way to the coroner's office. The team loaded up on coffee and headed for autopsy. Jennifer finished her coffee and began the exam.

"How can you guys eat and drink while Jennifer does an autopsy?" Angie said as she left her coffee outside the coroner's office.

"It's part of the job and you learn to eat and drink while you can," Cooper said laughing.

"That's gross," Angie said.

Jennifer followed her normal protocol in processing the body. This time she fingerprinted the victim first, in order to get the prints running through the computer while she worked. This was the first victim that was unknown at this stage of the investigation. She continued her normal process using the microscope, removing layers of clothes and repeating the process. When the clothes were removed Jennifer began washing the body.

During her exam, she noted that the victim had not been raped, sodomized, or bitten. She began to doubt that this was another of the serial killers victims until she found the wounds in her back. She saw a stab wound administered from behind that penetrated the layers of clothing. The victim had been placed face down on the ground and cut until the letter L formed into her back. This puncture was not as precise, but might be attributed to having more layers to puncture.

"The victim's right arm is broken," Jennifer said. "Her arm sustained a spiral fracture. This occurs when a bone is twisted too far and can't handle the force applied. The bone breaks in a spiral pattern up the bone rather than across as in a normal break."

"That must have been incredibly painful," Angie said.

"It would be," Jennifer said. "This victim did not have any bite marks on her body either. Layers of dirt were recovered from under her fingernails. Judging by her clothing and filth, she was probably homeless, but the scrapings from her nails will be sent to the state crime lab. The victim died around 1:30 am."

Jennifer removed the note from the body. This note was longer than the rest. It read, "She tried to rob me as I walked, she demanded all my cash. I broke her arm to prove a point, it happened in a flash. I hadn't planned to kill today, until she saw my face. I picked out my number seven, but now she's in her place. Having to kill her was not so fun, but now I'm on to number eight."

Prior to her death Carol hid in the alley awaiting an unsuspecting drunk staggering out of the bar. She peered around the corner and saw a small man heading her way.

"This'll be easy," she thought to herself.

She grabbed the man as he walked past her, dragging him into the alley. She held a broken piece of glass out towards him.

"Give me your wallet and you won't get hurt," she demanded. "And while you're at it, that's a nice watch."

He reached into his jacket to retrieve his wallet. He held the billfold out to her. As she reached forward, he quickly grabbed her wrist and twisted until he felt a snap. She dropped the broken glass.

"You broke my arm you bastard," she said clutching her damaged arm.

He spun her around and before she resisted, plunged the knife through her clothes and into her heart. She fell to the ground and rapidly bled out.

He struggled to make a vertical cut through her clothes. He made a second cut horizontally from the base of the first. He pulled the pen and notepad from his pocket and began to write. When he finished, he angrily shoved the note into her hand causing her arm to bend at an unnatural angle. He went to the nearby pay phone and made a call before walking off into the dark.

***

The CSPT report was in for the last two victims. Sheina's report was consistent with the coroner's report. The report on the homeless girl said that the victim had been found in an alley full of trash with an abundance of used drug paraphernalia in the area of the body. They didn't find an ID for this victim and were awaiting the autopsy print results. She was not tied up, but the stab wound was similar to the other victims. This victim appeared to be homeless and was not in the same physical condition as the others. They estimated her age to be in the mid 30's, but could not give an accurate age if the victim was a longtime drug user.

Cooper received a text that the fingerprints produced a hit and to check his email for a report on the victim. He opened the email and called his team together.

Cooper began his career when he was 23 years old. He graduated from college and began applying for law enforcement jobs. To Cooper they were not job interviews, but rather career interviews.

After applying for several agencies in the state, he received a job offer from the Seattle Police Department. Cooper began his career as a patrol officer. He graduated number one in a class of 150 new officers.

He was intelligent and quickly took to police work. He proved he was a shining star among the officers with even more experience. He ended up being the best partner Brooks worked with. No one from the police department knew about his famous film past.

"The victim's name is Carroll Clark, age 27, born July 7," Cooper told the team. "She ran away from home 12 years ago and was caught and fingerprinted. At the time she was listed as a runaway, she was living in California with her parents. Over the past five years, police arrested her several times for possession of methamphetamine (Meth) and prostitution here in Seattle. She always negotiated a lenient sentence by giving the drug task force information resulting in arrests of other drug users and dealers."

"Being a snitch may have caused her death," Brooks said.

"I don't think so," Cooper said. "She hasn't been arrested for six months and her death is too similar to our case."

Carroll's information was still current and her parents were contacted.

"Mr. and Mrs. Clark, I am Detective Cooper."

"What can we do for you officer," they asked.

"I am afraid that your daughter was found deceased this morning," Cooper said.

"Was it an overdose?" they asked.

"No, I'm afraid she was murdered," Cooper said.

"What happened to her?" Carroll's mother asked.

"She was attacked in an alley and stabbed to death, ma'am," Cooper said.

"Officer, I hate to sound heartless, but this is almost a relief," Carroll's father said.

"I don't understand," said Cooper.

"We lost track of her for the past several years and she's probably better off now than living on the streets," Mrs. Clark said.

"Like my husband said, it sounds heartless, but we've spent so many nights waiting for this call that we've aged by twenty years or more. Now we know our baby girl is not being abused or suffering on the streets."

"Each time we spoke to her we tried to convince her to come home and go into treatment," Carroll's father said. "We offered her a better life on numerous occasions, but the daughter we knew was too lost to be helped. We finally realized we couldn't help her unless she was ready to accept the help. The last time she spoke to us, we told her she was welcome to come home anytime. We would bring her home from anywhere if she agreed to be drug free. She was angry with us and hung up the phone. We never heard from her again. We are obviously heartbroken but relieved we found our daughter and she won't suffer any more. We've assumed for a long time that she was dead and now you confirmed our fears."

Brooks walked off and out of the office, while Cooper sat in the chair next to the two women.

"This poor lost girl," said Angie. "It's so sad to see a life like this wasted to drugs."

"We need to find this guy," Cooper said. "He'll be moving on soon if we don't. If we don't get a break soon, we'll fail the families, the victims, the community, and ourselves. This is not acceptable."

If they found the common link in the case, they had a better chance of predicting his next move and being ready to intercept him.

"Son of a bitch!" Brooks yelled in frustration from the hallway. He walked back in. "This girl is the same age as my daughter."

Brooks met his wife, Janet, 30 years ago when they were both 23, and they were married two years later. Their daughter, Lexi was still in college studying to be a physician's assistant, and was their only child. After ten years of Brooks being married to the job, Janet left him. They remained friends and were able to raise their daughter together from separate homes. Brooks dated off and on, but couldn't maintain a long-term relationship due to the dedication to his career.

He counted his blessings for the relationship between himself and his ex-wife. They were always able to put their daughter first or she could have easily fallen through the cracks and ended up on the streets like Carroll.

CHAPTER 19

The team ended the day no closer to catching the killer than before. None of them felt like having a drink and headed home for the night. When Brooks and Angie arrived at his house, they walked in and ran into Pam sitting in Brooks' favorite chair. She obviously didn't expect him to have another woman with him. He and Angie saw the expression of surprise on her face. Angie made an excuse to go to the bathroom while Brooks talked to Pam. While she was in the bathroom Angie listened to Brooks' telling Pam about the condominium incident and that she needed somewhere to stay.

"We are on the serial killer task force together," Brooks said.

"You don't owe me an explanation," Pam said. "I understood and I am supposed to be out of town for a month anyway. Do you mind introducing me to Angie?"

"I would be glad too," Brooks said.

Angie took this as her cue and exited the bathroom.

In the living room, Brooks' introduced the two women and offered them a drink on the deck. The women went outside and talked while he mixed the drinks. By the time he came out they were talking about him.

"He likes to walk around and flaunt himself," Pam said.

"Brooks is sly at finding an opportune moment to make a quiet but embarrassing statement too," Angie said with an understanding smile.

"He's a good kisser too," Pam said.

"I wouldn't know about that," Angie half-heartedly denied.

Brooks began to turn red and said they should change the subject.

"It might have been a bad idea to give either of you backup to get even with me," Brooks said.

Over the next hour, the two women did everything to embarrass Brooks. Since he knew he deserved it, he sat and took his punishment.

"You two are not always going to be around to have each-others back," Brooks said. "When I see a chance, I'll get even with you both."

He was also hoping he would get another chance to prove to Angie the comment about his kissing ability. She was thinking the same thing.

"I need to go. I'm still supposed to be out of town," Pam said. She hugged Angie and headed towards the door saying, "This time I won't be back for at least a month.

"I've heard that before," Brooks said as he walked her out.

"I have to leave for Japan in the morning," she gazed at him slyly and said, "I won't be in your way anytime soon."

She peered over his shoulder at Angie on the deck.

He rolled his eyes and said, "Call when you get back."

He and Angie went to their separate beds and went to sleep. At midnight, both their phones rang.

"Another body has been found and this one's not a woman," the dispatcher said. "But he did have a stab wound and a letter cut into him. The CSPT has already been dispatched and are on scene to process. You don't need to respond, but the chief asked that you be notified."

The two met in the hallway after the phone call and contemplated whether to go to the office or the scene.

"Should we go in?" asked Angie.

"We can't do anything until CSPT is done so we may as well try to get some rest," Brooks said.

By 5 am, they were unable to sleep. Angie jumped in the shower while Brooks made coffee. After arriving at the office they were met within a half hour by Cooper and Jennifer.

"The body's in my lab," Jennifer said.

Again, during the autopsy, Jennifer did not get any evidence from the microscopic view, the body wash, or the filter. They hoped to get something new from this body. The clothes were removed and Brooks stared at the victims face. He recognized this victim. He talked to him several days ago.

"I think that's Zumwalt, the volunteer I interviewed a few days ago," Brooks said.

Jennifer studied the paperwork and verified Brook's thought.

"It is Chad Zumwalt. I don't know him," Jennifer said.

She began her exam of the body and found no evidence until she turned him face down.

"Oh, my gosh," Angie said.

"What does that mean?" Cooper asked.

The team discovered he had been stabbed in the heart from behind like the others, but had more than a letter in his back. The killer used many small capital letters this time, spelling out, "THANKS."

"Does that mean the killer is done and we missed him," Brooks asked.

"We don't know yet," Cooper said. "Let's not jump to conclusions."

Jennifer concluded the exam by bringing out the note. This time it read, "This is how I found the girls, he gave me quite a list. He hates woman as much as I, isn't that a twist. I hadn't planned to kill him, he could have been huge help, when I stabbed him through the heart, he didn't even yell. He was not my friend, but a pawn I planned to frame, now his death provides him with a little bit of fame. You've made it fun for me my friend, it's been quite a ride. If you'd caught me before now, many would not have died."

The CSPT finished processing the scene at Zumwalt's house. Their reports would not be done for hours.

"I'll dig deeper into Zumwalt's life and see what turns up," Brooks said.

He was soon shocked to find that Zumwalt's mother passed away several years ago.

"Whom did I talk to on the phone? Was it Zumwalt or the killer?" Brooks asked himself. "I guess we may never know unless we catch the killer."

Cooper requested Zumwalt's police computer records to determine if he retrieved the victim's names from department computers while doing his volunteer hours.

"I've got his computer files," Cooper said. "Zumwalt attended a training class on photo lineups. During that training, he learned that a police officer can input information about a suspect and the driver's license bureau will email a list of people matching the description. This may have been how Zumwalt compiled a list of woman of a certain height and weight. This also allowed him to get addresses and phone numbers on woman who registered to vote while renewing their license."

"That little son of a bitch," Brooks said. "Guys like that give good cops a bad reputation."

Brooks checked the files that Zumwalt accessed and found what they feared.

"Zumwalt printed out a list of about two hundred woman matching the same characteristics as our current victims," Brooks said.

Brooks printed the list.

"All the victims are on this list," Brooks said. "There are a lot of other names on this list with birthdays still to come. The killer has never repeated a month, and is going in order so far. If the killer keeps progressing through the months, the list of potential victims is down to 58 women. This may be a huge break for the case."

"The Crime Scene Processing Team finished Zumwalt's house late in the night," Angie said. "They returned early this morning to complete reports. Once they finish, the reports will be delivered to our office. These reports might shed even more light on the killer."

Angie read the CSPT report to the team.

"They recovered only Zumwalt's fingerprints in the residence. All other possible prints found were smudges and unable to be used. They also found a case of Tyvek suits in the living room, but only one suit is left in a box of 40. They found two bedrooms of the house were being used and Zumwalt's police uniform and badge are missing."

"Also," Angie continued. "Zumwalt owned a set of five knives with a single sided blade and a serrated blade for the last .75 of an inch. One knife was used to compare to molds of the puncture wounds of the current victims. The knives matched. They were similar to a copy of the knife previously found, but were manufactured by a Montana knife maker. The brand on the knife said Morin Knives. They also found the missing items from the first couple of girls. Zoe's charm bracelet, Chandra's necklace with the locket, Janelle's heart shaped ring, and Julie's picture in the frame. The small items were located in a space under a floorboard in Zumwalt's room. They compared Zumwalt's throw rug with the fibers on Chandra and they matched. They speculated that the throw rug was Chandra's and Zumwalt kept it as a trophy. They also checked Zumwalt's truck for a match to the tire impressions at the college. The left rear tire matched the pattern found at the scene."

"The report further indicated that a call came from Zumwalt's residence at 5:32 p.m. and the phone went dead," Angie read.

Standard procedure was for the police to respond to 911 hang up calls to verify everything was okay.

"The responding officer spotted Zumwalt on the floor by the front door," Angie said. "He only went in far enough to check for a pulse before backing out of the house. The officer called for backup, and they searched the residence for other victims and secured the perimeter of the residence. CSPT ended their search by swabbing areas most likely to have DNA and the swabs were sent to the FBI lab."

"I'll bet this bastard's been wearing the uniform to get into the apartments," Brooks said. "I think he put the Tyvek suit on once he was inside. It's no wonder we haven't been finding much evidence from the killer. He's much smarter than I thought."

Before the team completed reading the reports, they were told of another body discovered this morning. Brooks grabbed the list and he and Jennifer responded to the scene while Cooper and Angie continued with the reports.

When Brooks and Jennifer arrived, they found the victim to be Dana Hansen born August 25.

"Dana's 20 years old, living alone in a two bedroom apartment," the dispatcher said. "We received an anonymous call again."

Dana was half-asleep when the knock on the door came. She answered the door in her pajamas.

"What are you wearing?" she asked, letting the man in the apartment.

"I want to try something different tonight," the man said.

He removed her pajamas and tied her hands behind her back. When they were done having sex, he tied her feet together. He laid her on her back and began to bite her several times until she asked him to stop.

"That hurts and isn't fun for me," she said.

"Can I try a couple more things?" he asked.

"Okay but it better not hurt," Dana said.

He turned her over and gently massaged her back. She relaxed a little and he forced the knife through her skin and into her heart. She tried to gasp. She glared over her shoulder at him as if to say, "What have you done?" and her life was over. He made his cuts in her back and cleaned up for work.

***

They ran Dana's name and date of birth through the in car computer and found a speeding ticket in the past, but no known arrests. As they were getting ready to leave, they caught sight of an upset man attempting to get past the police tape, screaming Dana's name.

Brooks grabbed the man and asked his name.

"My name's Clayton Boyd.

"How old are you?" Brooks asked.

"I'm 35," Boyd said as he gave his date of birth.

"Do you know Dana and what can you tell me about her?" Brooks asked.

"I met Dana while I was getting a massage and we've dated since," Boyd said. "I don't know anything about Dana's family. We've talked about them and I got the impression that she didn't get along with her family so I didn't press the issue."

"Do you have access to her apartment?" Brooks asked.

"I don't have a key but she lets me in if that's what you mean. I don't live here, but I spend the night from time to time.

"Can I ask what happened," Boyd said.

"Dana was killed by an intruder," Brooks said.

Clayton appeared confused and surprised but not sad.

"When did it happen? Who would do such a horrible thing to her?" Boyd asked.

While interviewing Boyd, they remarked to each other that he wore gloves on his hands. These gloves were the type a burn victim would wear if his hands were burned and he was healing. They were tan in color with pores in them to allow breathing of the skin while his burns healed. Boyd saw them glancing at his hands.

"I burned both my hands with chemicals," Boyd said. "I work in the local foundry and put my hands down on a tray that contained acid. The tray appeared to be empty and shouldn't have contained acid where the accident occurred."

"Is it painful," Brooks asked.

"At first, but isn't too bad now."

"We can't allow you to go in the residence until the investigation is over," Brooks said. "While we're here, do you have an ID I can use to write down your information?"

"I don't have my ID with me," Boyd said.

Brooks and Jennifer asked all the questions they needed for his information and released Boyd.

"Can someone call me when I can gather my things from the

apartment?" Boyd asked.

Brooks and Jennifer found this question to be odd for someone who found out his girlfriend died. They left CSPT at the scene with special instructions to pay attention to any male property and relayed the boyfriends comment.

While driving to meet the other members of the team for lunch, Jennifer scanned Zumwalt's list.

"Dana's name is on page two of Zumwalt's list," Jennifer said.

She began to mark the names of anyone born between September and December on the list.

"We only have 42 names left with birthdays still coming," Jennifer said.

At lunch, the four compared notes from the current scene and from Zumwalt's house. Jennifer relayed the information about Boyd and the team agreed to go over his life with a fine-toothed comb.

CHAPTER 20

While they were still eating, the team was notified that Deltin had been found.

"Two officers followed him home and set up a perimeter on his house," dispatch said.

"The address sounds familiar," Brooks said.

As they went through the paperwork, they found that Deltin lived near the apartment complex where Ashley Long lived. Angie took the warrant on Deltin to the judge and he signed it. This would not only allow them to arrest Deltin on his warrant but also allow them to search his residence, car, and any other property that Deltin owned.

"I'm calling a press conference to announce that the serial killer is being arrested today," the chief said.

"I wouldn't say anything until we confirm Deltin is the right suspect," Brooks said.

"Leave the press to the professional and do your jobs," the chief said.

While they were preparing to serve the warrant, the chief was on television.

"My team found the serial killer. They are arresting the suspect as we speak. I'm appreciative for the ability to put an excellent team together."

The chief carried on taking credit for the arrest of Deltin and closing the serial killer case.

Brooks and Cooper contacted the warrant service team.

"We have a warrant that needs to be served now," Brooks said. "He's an unregistered sex offender and may be our serial killer."

"You got it," said the warrant service commander.

Within the hour, the team was stationed outside of Deltin's house. They used four officers in the front and three officers in the back. One officer was stationed to the south and west side, while another officer set up on the north and east side of the residence.

The commander gave the signal, "Go."

The officers tactically approached the front and back door. The team knocked on the front and back door at the same time and announced they were the police with a warrant.

This was a new case law requirement in the past few years. The law said an officer should announce his presence and that he has a warrant. The officer must give a reasonable amount of time to answer the door before breaking it down.

Many people felt this was another procedure that gave suspects the upper hand. This gave them time to destroy evidence and arm themselves. Several officers were already shot while waiting at the door and several others were shot while entering to serve a warrant.

The officers waited a reasonable amount of time and breeched the front and back door simultaneously. As they entered, a fearful Deltin came running out of a back room. When he saw the police, he locked the door he exited and put his hands up.

"Get on the ground," said the lead officer.

He was handcuffed and escorted out of the house.

"You can't search the house," Deltin screamed. "You have no right to search the house."

Angie walked up with a smile and put a copy of the search and arrest warrants in Deltin's shirt.

"If you search my house," Deltin said. "I'll sue you."

Most of the search was uneventful. The search team found some paperwork that indicated Deltin owned a nearby storage unit, but nothing that linked him to the homicides. Then they reached the locked room. They kicked the door open and cautiously entered. They searched the room and were about to leave when an officer spotted dirt on the carpet in the closet and a dirty pair of shoes.

"There's a line of dirt on the carpet that doesn't look right," the officer said. "I found a door here."

They opened the door and saw it led to the crawl space below the house. Two officers entered the crawl space with guns drawn.

"It's not a crawl space," said the officer. "There are several rooms with dirt floors down here."

They waited for two more officers and entered the first room. This room contained two tables with restraint devices on each. One table was padded with a pillow at the head of the table. The other table was solid wood with restraints in the corners. On the wall were numerous sexual aids, toys and large wooden boxes on the floor.

The officers entered the second room to find a small blindfolded woman restrained to a bed. The woman was nude and obviously abused. She had welts and marks all over her body and severe bruising on her wrists and ankles from the restraints. The woman was crying, but heard someone in the room.

"Please don't hurt me," she said. "I can't take anymore."

"Police ma'am, we're here to help you," the officer said. "Don't be afraid, we are going to untie you."

The officers removed the blindfold and called for medics to the residence.

"Let the medics know you're coming and take this woman out to the ambulance," the officer said.

After the woman was gone, the search team began to search in the boxes on the floor.

"All three boxes contain bones," the officer said.

The officers completed the search and briefed Brooks and his team.

"We recovered three bodies in boxes downstairs," the officer said. "Deltin has his own torture chamber too."

They turned the house over to CSPT for processing. The search team informed the task force of the storage unit receipt they recovered. Angie amended her warrant and phoned the judge. The judge recorded the conversation and gave Angie a verbal signature for her warrant, also known as a telephonic warrant. The warrant team and the task force were at the storage unit by the time the telephonic warrant was signed. The warrant team entered the storage unit and cleared it for suspects. After the area was secure, the task force team searched the unit.

"Judging by the pictures in here," Brooks said, "Deltin became more violent after his conviction. He got better at hiding his sick fetish."

"He's got a file cabinet full of pornographic material," Angie said. "Most of this is depicting bondage and torture. He also has two photo albums of missing children fliers, with part of the book marked "Marvin's toys." Sixteen fliers are in this section."

As the team searched boxes and containers in the unit, they found most of the items were Deltin's personal belongings. They approached the larger containers stacked in the corner.

"Oh my God," Angie said.

"There's a small body in here. It's only bones, but they are small. You guys check the other three containers."

"He has a body in each container," Brooks said after checking.

The team finished the search and left the bodies as they found them so the CSPT processed an undisturbed the scene. CSPT needed to process Dana's apartment, Deltin's house, his car, and now his storage unit. With only three CSPT teams on staff, they were all called out to help. The task force would start fresh in the morning.

By the morning, all three scenes and reports were complete. The task force would spend the day making sense of what they discovered and what the CSPT recovered. Each task force member took a report.

Angie read the report from Dana's apartment. The team at Dana's residence found similar things as in many other scenes. Again, they found no signs of forced entry. No fingerprints accept those belonging to the victim. The victim had been stabbed from behind while lying face down and cut forming the letter Y. Her hands were tied behind her back before her death, and her feet were tied together later. She did not have the amount of marks on her hands and feet as the other victims. She was either tied up later or did not struggle with the bindings as much.

"Some differences were found in this case," Angie told the team. "She had been sexually active but didn't appear to be raped, but this victim suffered four distinct bite marks on her abdomen. She had one bite below each breast and one bite above and below her navel. She also had a sheet placed over her after her death. The note in her right-hand read, "After killing number eight, I am feeling fine. I guess that means I'm ready, to go on to number nine."

"The sheet placement usually means remorse or shame on the part of the killer," Brooks said. "He attempted to cover his actions with someone he cared about. He doesn't want this person left in the open to be found by anyone passing by. This may be an important indicator of some type of relationship between the victim and killer. Although he may have felt some remorse, it obviously wasn't enough to prevent killing her."

Cooper read the report from Deltin's home.

"The crime scene team recovered evidence that dated back twenty years," Cooper said. "Deltin collected child pornography since his late teens. The team found hundreds of photos of girls from 14-17 in his file cabinet and throughout his house. Many of the photos appeared to have been taken by Deltin himself. In the basement, they found the three bodies in the boxes. Inside each box was a missing child flier of a juvenile between 14 and 17 years of age. DNA samples were sent to the FBI lab for comparison with samples being provided by parents of the missing children on the fliers.

"Those poor families," Angie said.

"The woman alive in the basement was later identified as a 16-year-old runaway," Cooper said. "She's currently at the hospital being examined and her parents are with her. The processing team did not find anything in Deltin's home that would link him to the current homicides."

"That's what I was afraid of," Brooks said.

Jennifer read the next report."In Deltin's car the team recovered multiple blood samples from the carpet in the trunk. The samples are being sent to the FBI lab for DNA analysis. Carpet samples were taken from the car and none matched the samples from the fibers found in our serial killer case."

"The chief's gonna look like an ass," Brooks said.

"You tried to warn him," Jennifer said.

"In the glove box of the car, they found sixteen ID's matching the fliers in Deltin's book," Jennifer said. The living victim's ID' is among them. This means that he held at least eight more ID's than known victims. The vehicle is being held at the local crime lab in case further processing is needed."

"I bet he's killed the other fifteen girls," Cooper said.

Brooks received the report from the storage unit.

"Inside the unit, the processing team recovered thousands of photos of underage girls in compromising positions," Brooks read aloud. "Many of the girls in the photos did not appear to be comfortable and even appeared scared. They found other photos showing women being tied up and tortured. They could not determine if the women were with Deltin voluntarily or not. The processors also found four containers with skeletons in them."

"The same four we found or four more?" asked Angie.

"No, the same four we found," Brooks said. "Each container held a missing child flier that may identify the victim. The team also took DNA samples to send to the FBI lab, and requested the parents supply items that might contain their daughter's DNA. This would include hairbrushes, toothbrushes, clothing, or baby teeth, anything the family still kept that contained DNA. This team did not find anything linking Deltin to the current serial killer case."

After reading the reports and briefing each other on the evidence, they decided to split up. Jennifer helped examine the bones of the victims, and Angie accompanied her. Cooper and Brooks were going to ascertain if Deltin was willing to be interviewed now. They would meet back in the task force office later to discuss what they found.

CHAPTER 21

Cooper and Brooks met with Deltin. They remarked to each other that he seemed defeated and dejected. He appeared sad, with his head hanging down towards his chest, he refused to make eye contact, he sighed heavily and his voice sounded small and feeble. When he was introduced to the officers, he would not look them in the eye and was barely audible when asked if he heard them. He was read his Miranda rights and Deltin said he understood. The officers excused themselves to retrieve copies of the photos of the skeletons as well as a photo of the live victim. They returned 45 minutes later, and Deltin's demeanor did not change. He was sitting in the same position. He acted as if a doctor told him he would only live a few days.

"Do you still understand your rights," Brooks asked.

"Yes, I remember and understand," Deltin mumbled softly.

"Can you tell us what's been happening in your house," Brooks asked.

"I've been abducting girls for almost two decades," Deltin said. "I took one at a time and played with them for almost a year. It started innocently. I ran across a child that I recognized from a missing person flier. I offered her a safe place to live and free food if she cleaned my house and she agreed. Once I got her home I stuck to the deal."

"As time went on with the first girl, I wanted more and more from her until I came to a point where I needed to have sex," Deltin confessed. "We began to have sex and it was originally consensual. As my sexual desires became kinkier, she began to turn me down. I eventually demanded she perform things she wasn't willing to do. That's when something in me snapped."

"After she refused to perform for me, I began to tie her up and do what I wanted anyway," Deltin said. "When I finished, I would keep her in a closet where no one would hear her. I eventually got tired of her and smothered her. I abducted someone once a year after that and ended up with sixteen young girls, over almost two decades."

Brooks and Cooper sat stone-faced, while they felt like unleashing a torrent of internal fury on him.

"I began to search for rental houses with a crawl space after the first two girls," Deltin said. "I got more and more violent with each one until I reached a point where sex wasn't enough, I needed to abuse and torture them to reach the same level of arousal. With each young woman, I pushed the envelope until she reached a breaking point. Once they broke, they were no longer any fun. I kept them until I found a new toy to play with. Once I found a replacement, I would kill the last victim."

"I started by smothering the first one and as I collected more and more victims I found it exciting to kill them with new and different violent ways," Deltin stated. "When I did this in front of the new victim, they were much more compliant right away rather than fighting me."

Cooper and Brooks saw that reliving this gave Deltin a new sense of energy. He was talking in an excited fashion, and was now using hand gestures and was animated. He was obviously reliving the moments with each of the victims as he described it in gut wrenching detail. Deltin began to view the photos of the young women.

"I remember everything I did to each one and exactly where I put them," Deltin said. "I know I'm looking at the death penalty and will tell you where the other bodies are if you don't try to execute me.

"That's up to the prosecutor," said Brooks. "But if you are totally honest with us, we'll try to make it happen. Not for you, but for the families of the victims still missing."

Over the next three hours, Deltin wrote in detail the events that occurred to end the girl's lives. By the time he finished he had written seven pages of confession, admitting to all sixteen girl's deaths. He admitted he knew where the remaining bodies where, but would not say until he was guaranteed he would not be executed. Deltin concluded his statements by admitting that the fliers inside the containers and boxes were the bones of the missing girls. He said that when he took them to the other bodies, missing person fliers were buried with them as well.

The officers concluded the interview by going over the written statement and clarifying anything confusing or unclear. Deltin was proud of what he had done and wanted everyone to know in detail, how he escaped the law for so long. He was looking forward to being famous and obviously didn't care why.

"Is it legal to make money off my crime when they want to make a movie of my life," Deltin asked.

"Under Washington law, someone convicted of a crime is not allowed to profit from that crime," Brooks said gladly. "You won't receive a dime."

This crushed his pride and deflated his smug attitude about killing the girls.

The team met up to discuss the day.

"We're done with the bones," Jennifer relayed. "We determined that many of the girls were beaten to death because of trauma to the skull and neck bones. Many of the girls showed signs of healing broken bones at the time of their deaths. The measurements of the bones are consistent with the size of the girl listed on the attached flier."

This meant it was possible for the flier to be with the actual missing girl in question. The men relayed the events of the interview with Deltin. The women were shocked by what he said and did to those poor girls.

"Will the prosecutor still go for the death penalty?" Angie asked.

"I spoke to the prosecutor and he won't ask for the death penalty unless all the family members of the missing girls wanted him too," Brooks said.

As they were finishing the briefing, the chief called them into his office.

"You guys made me look like a fool on TV today," the chief said. "What new information do you have?"

They briefed him of what had been transpiring.

"I'll make a call and ascertain if we can expedite the DNA processing," the chief said. "If we can get things going, we might have DNA reports back within a day or two."

The team left his office and broke for the day.

Brooks and Angie sat on the deck drinking rum and coke. The ferryboats moved back and forth from Seattle to Bremerton. They didn't get the sense of calm previously enjoyed. They were too traumatized by what they witnessed and heard to feel relief. They felt a sense of victory for catching a serial killer, but not the one they sought. They were still digesting Deltin's information and the injuries to the live victims, as well as seeing seven sets of young girl's bones in boxes, as if it was a present to someone. Brooks realized they didn't investigate Clayton Boyd. He called the nightshift detectives and asked that they compile any information they can find on him.

When they arrived the next day, the chief had been true to his word.

"I called the FBI lab last night and the DNA is being worked on today. "The reports will be faxed in the evening," the chief said.

Jennifer and Angie headed to the hospital to interview the living victim and speak to her parents, while Cooper and Brooks read the night detective's reports on Boyd.

When the two women arrived at the hospital room, the victim's parents met them. Angie showed them a photo of Deltin and asked if they recognized him.

"He performed some yard work for us almost a year ago, but we stopped using him because he kept leering in the bedroom windows when we were changing," the mother said. "He would be in the front of the house when we went to our rooms to change, but he would appear outside the window on the side of the house and pretend to be working on something a few minutes later. We fired him because I thought he was trying to catch us without clothes on.

"When did you fire him?" Angie asked.

"About three months before our daughter disappeared," she said.

Angie spoke to the victim.

"Can you tell me your name?" Angie asked.

"Jodie Garcia," she said.

"Are you up to talking to us now?" Angie asked.

"I'll try," she said.

"Do you know the name of the man who abducted you?" Angie said.

"Mr. Deltin is what he made me call him," she said. "I don't know if that's his real name."

"Can you tell us what happened in the house where we found you?" Angie asked.

"Mr. Deltin held me captive for four months and abused me the entire time. He would allow me to come upstairs to cook and clean, but never allowed me to leave. He always tied me up before he left and I never felt safe enough to escape. Mr. Deltin threatened to kill my family if I left.

Her mother broke down when she heard this new information.

Mrs. Garcia, can you please step out," Jennifer asked. "You don't need to know all the details. You need to appreciate that she's okay."

Mrs. Garcia left the room.

"It began when he brought me into the crawl space where they found me," Jodie said. "Another girl was in rough shape when I arrived. The other girl was beaten and barely alive, but Mr. Deltin would untie her and make her dig to expand the room below the house. After several days of being tied up, Mr. Deltin moved me into the same room as the other girl, and tortured, and beat that girl to death. That's why I was afraid to ever say no to Mr. Deltin or try to escape."

After killing her Mr. Deltin made me start working," Jodie said. "I cooked, cleaned and attended to his every whim, including having sex with him. During sex he was aggressive and liked to punish me with whips and other items. Mr. Deltin got some joy out of making me afraid and in pain."

"Are you still okay to talk to us?" Angie asked.

"I want this over," Garcia said.

"Okay please continue," Angie said.

"Mr. Deltin would get more excited with each torturous thing he did to me until he couldn't hold out any longer and forced me to have sex with him," Jodie said. "Mr. Deltin always told me that if I continued to cooperate I would not see the same fate as the last victim. I cooperated as much as possible, but sometimes the beating and torture were too much. I asked him to stop, and that would make him more upset. He would beat me more. My cries ruined his enjoyment when I asked him to stop."

"Do you need to take a break?" asked Angie. "I understand this is difficult."

"I need to get it out," Garcia said while lightly crying. "May I please continue?"

I'm sorry," Angie said. "Please go ahead."

"After Mr. Deltin killed the girl, he told me he buried her somewhere no one would find her. He told me not to worry, that he would bring her back someday. After about two months, he brought back a box with bones in it. He told me they were the bones of the girl I met in the basement. I saw Mr. Deltin put her in the box. He often came down in the basement and stared into the boxes. He would open them side-by-side and sit smiling. He would sit for about an hour staring into the boxes and by the time he was done, he was so sexually wound up he would begin the beating and torture that always led to some sort of sex."

As Angie and Jennifer completed the interview and walked away, they both felt sick to their stomachs. They didn't want to talk in the car or even talk about the case anymore. They wanted this case to be over and never discuss it again. Jennifer reached into her pocket and turned off the recorder.

CHAPTER 22

Cooper and Brooks began to go over Clayton Boyd's history. What they found was interesting. According to the other detective's report, Boyd did not exist until about two and a half years ago. Prior to that time, he had no bills, phone records, rental agreements, homeownership papers, credit cards, or any type of history on Clayton Lee Boyd II. He didn't exist until two and a half year ago and he's now 35 years old, born 10-14-79. Prior to that time, he did not exist anywhere in the world. He popped up two and a half years ago, with a New York Driver's license. The detective was able to find paperwork in Boyd's name in Tennessee and Colorado. The most recent information was a motel credit card purchase for the Red Lion in Seattle from November 30 to December 10. For the last week, he fell off the grid, made no purchases, and didn't access his bank accounts. They did not have a current address, vehicles registered to him, or any family at all, much less in the area. It also appeared that Boyd did not own a cell phone. The detectives report concluded saying that Boyd was like a ghost who appears and disappears at will.

That afternoon some of the FBI DNA reports came in.

"We've gotten some of the DNA results back guys," Brooks said.

"Don't keep it to yourself, what's it say?" Cooper asked.

"The DNA from Deltin's car matched the DNA from the three sets of bones in his basement," Brooks said. "The DNA from the bones also matched the girls in the boxes except two fliers were placed in the wrong boxes. They've already notified the prosecutor."

"I'm charging Deltin with sixteen counts of deliberate homicide," the state prosecutor said." I'm also charging him with sixteen counts of felony child abuse, and sixteen counts of rape of a child. I'm going to ask that Deltin be sentenced to life without parole."

This means that Deltin would not be executed, but would die in prison with no possibility of ever being released.

"I came to this conclusion after several parents asked that Deltin's life be spared so they could find the body of their child for burial," said the prosecutor. "Deltin will be sent to a protective custody unit of the state prison where he'll serve his time with other violent sexual offenders."

Deltin was given these conditions and agreed to show where he buried the other bodies. If he followed through, he would serve his sentence without the possibility of execution, but also without freedom.

Deltin supplied addresses to three previous houses he rented and the task force began to write warrants for those houses. Deltin gave detailed descriptions of where each body was buried under each house and how deep. A judge signed the warrants and the warrant service team served them. Once the residences were secured, the CSPT processed the crawl spaces to locate the bodies.

The Warrant Service Team served the warrants without issue. The CSPT teams were able to locate eight bodies in boxes buried in the dirt in the crawl spaces of Deltin's previous rentals. Each box contained a full set of bones as well as a missing child flier. The team was able to use the teeth of the victims for comparison since they most likely already had their identity. Each set of parents eagerly provided the dental records of their child for identification purposes. Each child was verified as the child listed on the fliers from the box. Deltin, true to his word, would now be in prison until he died. The DNA from the first two crimes scenes would not return for a couple more days.

While they were all together, the chief made an announcement.

"The prosecutor finished his review of Cooper and Brook's shooting incident," the chief said. "The prosecutor found the shooting incident to be a justifiable homicide under the laws of the State of Washington. This means no charges will be filed against you and the prosecutor will present the case that way to the inquest."

"I told you not to worry," Angie said.

"Everything worked out as it should have months ago," Jennifer said.

"As far as the department and the family are concerned the incident is over and no further actions against you is necessary," the chief said. "You may still have to go into a coroner's inquest."

Cooper and Brooks both thought that after the prosecutor reviewed the facts of the case and determined he was not going to file charges against the officers, the case would be labeled a justifiable homicide and sealed. They've never heard of a case being cleared by the prosecutor that didn't clear the coroner's inquest.

The coroner's inquest was like a trial. The officers and any other witnesses would explain what they saw and what happened from their own perspective. The prosecutor would lead the trial by asking questions of the witnesses and officers on the stand. The trial consists of a judge and a six-person panel of jurors from the community. The jurors would listen to the facts of the case as presented by the prosecutor and would determine if the officers were justified in using lethal force, or if charges should be filed. The officers would only be called in if any doubts arose after questioning witnesses. The recommendations of the jurors would be given to the judge and he or she would have the ultimate say as to the outcome of the case.

Every officer involved shooting went through this process to ensure the department does not cover up the use of lethal force outside the guidelines of the law, as well as department policies. After several high profile cases nationwide, the coroner's inquest involved the community to make sure police follow the laws and policies set forth to protect the public from abuse. It was viewed as a measure of checks and balances.

Brooks and Cooper could now focus on this case and not worry about other outside problems. They still needed to wait a few weeks for the inquest.

"It's been quite a day," Brooks said.

"No kidding," Cooper said. "We were cleared in the shooting incident, we removed a serial killer and child molester from the streets for good, we gave some parents closure on their missing children and possibly identified the serial killer we're still after."

The task force went out for a celebratory drink at The Padded Cell. They toasted a tremendously uplifting day and hoped to carry that success forward.

As they celebrated, Cooper received a call.

"Hey Coop," an officer said. "I'm at your house and it has a car in the basement."

"What are you talking about?" Cooper asked.

"A car smashed into your house," the officer said. "The car damaged the main floor. The car ended up in the basement after traveling half way through the house before crashing through the floor. The driver fled and the vehicle is stolen."

Cooper left for home, but said, "I'll call you and let you know how bad it is."

The rest of the team stayed at the bar and tried to maintain their natural high.

About an hour later, Cooper called.

"The car destroyed the main floor of the house and half of the basement. The structure's compromised and I can't live at home or even go inside to get my clothes."

"Since you live close, you can stay with me until you find something more permanent, or your house can be rebuilt," Jennifer said.

Cooper agreed and came back to the bar. A construction crew worked on getting the car out and securing the house until an inspector examined it. The team ended the day on a positive note despite the devastation with Cooper's house. When Cooper and Jennifer left, Cooper swung by the house and snuck inside to get the essentials he needed. He arrived at Jennifer's house ninety minutes later.

"What took you so long?" Jennifer asked.

"I stopped by the house to get some things," Cooper said. "I loaded what I could from the house and put it in my truck."

"How's the house?" Jennifer asked.

"A little scary," Cooper said. "The floor was shaking under me as I walked and I thought for sure I would fall through. It didn't stop me from grabbing everything before the inspector says to demolish the house and everything in it."

They unloaded what he would need at Jennifer's and locked the rest inside the canopy of his truck. He turned on the alarm.

"I hope no one steals my truck," Cooper said.

"I'll move my car out and you can put your truck in the garage," Jennifer said.

They switched the cars around and went inside to talk about the day. As the night wore on, they talked about Brooks.

"Brooks is the best cop I've ever worked with," Cooper said. "I hope he sticks around until I'm ready to retire."

"It's nice having someone you can count on in your life," Jennifer said. "I miss having someone in my life when I need them."

"What am I chopped liver," Cooper said.

They laughed and she thought to herself, "Why not Cooper?"

"Why don't we head to bed," Jennifer said. "You can be what I need tonight as a start."

Cooper and Jennifer arrived together in the morning and made it no secret they spent the night together. Brooks glanced at her with a sly grin.

"I needed to release some aggression last night," Jennifer said. "Cooper was willing to be the victim."

"Yeah, I can show you the marks if you want proof," Cooper said proudly.

CHAPTER 23

"The officer took prints from the car in Cooper's house," Brooks said. "He printed the steering wheel before he was told to get out of the house because it may collapse. The prints were dropped at the lab last night and compared this morning. They matched the smudged prints from the first two crime scenes."

How's the killer know where you live?" Angie asked. "Why did he destroy your house?"

Was he stalking them or gotten lucky? The chief was notified and a surveillance specialist was sent to all their houses to set up video cameras.

"I already own a security system and don't need anyone to add more to my house," Brooks said. "I will review the recent footage and see if anything suspicious shows up."

He thought he heard an audible sigh of relief from Angie.

The team was notified of another body found in a second story apartment.

"The body was found when a cable installer came in to install a new line," the dispatcher said. "The victim's 24-year-old Mi Anne Gruber. Mi Anne was born in September and worked as a department store clerk. The cable installer and the landlord who let him in are being brought to the task force office by a patrol officer."

The landlord was interviewed and he was a fragile elderly man who did not have the power or energy to kill women this age. He was a WWII veteran who seemed un-phased by the incident. He said he had been home for the previous eight hours. With his alibi confirmed, he was released.

The cable installer was interviewed. He was on a job with six other installers running cable lines for a new business opening this week. He went straight from the business job to the apartment job.

He was clearly having trouble accepting what he discovered and kept saying, "It can't be real."

His alibi was confirmed and he was released back to work.

MI Anne expected the cable installer and landlord sometime today. She had already worked out and showered before they were scheduled to arrive. She was enjoying a fresh cup of coffee. She went to step out the door to get the newspaper the same time she did every day. This time she opened the door and a man was standing outside holding the newspaper. After a brief conversation, she let him in. She was not threatened or intimidated by the man at all. She offered him a cup of coffee and the officer declined.

"Have you had any problems in or around you apartment ma'am?" He asked.

"No, as far as I know everything is fine," she said.

"Have you seen any men hanging around that you are unfamiliar with?" he asked.

"No," Mi Anne said. "But I don't know the cable guy that's coming today."

"We caught a man peering into the second window from the front door," the officer said. "What room would that be?"

"Oh, my gosh, that's my bedroom," she said.

"Can you show me please," the officer said.

She showed him to the bedroom. He pointed out the window the man had been peering into. She walked past the officer to look out the window. He grabbed her from behind and threw her on the bed. He pinned her to the bed with his weight. Boyd showed her the knife.

"If you cooperate with me I won't hurt you," he said.

"What are you going to do?" she asked in fear.

She began to cry and this made him excited.

"Whatever I want darling," Boyd said.

He forced her hands behind her back and quickly tied them. He turned her over and initiated his sexual assault. She glared into his eyes and saw pure joy over what he was doing. She turned her face away and stared at a terrified woman next to the bed.

"Who is she?" she thought to herself.

She realized it was her own reflection in the mirror on the wall. He ended the assault by biting her numerous times around her breasts and stomach. He tied her feet and she tried to kick him. He blocked the kick and tied her feet even tighter. He turned her onto her stomach and again pinned her down with his weight.

He sat straddling her back listening to her struggle to breathe. Finally, he pushed the knife slowly through the skin on her back and into her heart. He waited several minutes for all movement to cease. Once her movement stopped, he began his precise cuts. When he completed his mission, he exited the apartment as a cable truck pulled into the parking lot.

***

The team met Jennifer in the coroner's office for the autopsy while they waited on the CSPT report. Jennifer followed her normal protocols and once again didn't find any fibers or evidence from the clothing or scan of the body. When examining Mi Anne's body she found that the stab wound was the same and the cut spelled out the letter D. She discovered signs of sexual assault and five bite marks. This time, one bite mark was below each breast, one three inches above the navel, and two below the navel. It almost seemed as if a smiley face was forming, with the upper bites making the eyes, the centered bite making the nose and the lower navel bites making the mouth.

The CSPT report came in after the autopsy, with a copy of the note. When they got to the note from her hand it read, "Now I've finished number nine, and on my way again. I'll have a surprise in store, when you find number ten." The rest of the report was similar to the others. No strange fibers, hairs or evidence were recovered at the scene. The victim died in the bedroom when she was stabbed through the heart. They found no signs of forced entry and no signs of how the killer exited, like the other scenes. No signs of a struggle were evident in the apartment and nothing was broken or misplaced.

The task force phone rang and Angie answered. She said yes a couple of times and stated she would be right down to let him in.

"A man in the lobby may have video of Dana's apartment," Angie said.

Angie brought the man to the task force office.

"What do you have for us?" Brooks asked.

"I have a video from my apartment," said the man, "I know that sounds creepy but I can explain. I live in the same apartment complex as Dana. Someone tampered with my car recently so I set up the camera in the curtain of my window facing the parking lot. After I heard about the murder, I thought the suspect may be on video since my camera faced Dana's area of the parking lot for the past week."

"Have you watched the tape?" asked Cooper.

"No, I haven't," he said.

They made copies of the video and released the man. They placed the original in evidence and began to view a copy.

The day of Dana's death, at 4:30 a.m. on the video, the team spotted a green Ford Escort pull into a visitor parking spot in front of the victim's apartment.

"Let's see where this guy goes," Angie said.

"Isn't that Boyd?" Jennifer said.

"He's wearing a police uniform," Cooper said. "He's at Dana's door knocking."

"Look, he's going inside," Brooks said.

They continue viewing the video.

"Here he comes," Cooper said. "He's been in the apartment for almost twenty-five minutes. He's wearing a Tyvek suit now, but he's got his police jacket on the top half where the blood would be."

They asked the surveillance specialist to enhance the video and find a license plate number on the vehicle. They also asked the auto theft division if any green Escorts were reported stolen lately. The auto theft officer pulled a file and found 12 stolen Escorts in the last month. Three of the vehicles were located so they were removed from the list. This still left nine possible vehicles if the killer was using a stolen car. Cooper received a list of license plates and forwarded a copy to the video enhancement specialist. He was notified to give them at least four hours to work their magic. He briefed the team and they began to examine their copy of the video again, but this time paying special attention to times before the incident. Did the suspect case the apartment one or two days before? As they watched the video, they felt a sense of hope now. If they identified the car, the killer would not know about the video and they may surprise him before any more deaths occurred. Boyd would not know that they possessed his driver's license, the vehicle he was driving, and fliers would be disbursed around the county.

The video enhancement specialist called.

"We received a match to a stolen license plate," he said. "It's a

Washington State license plate reported stolen three days ago from the parking area at pier 51, where one other victim died. The license plate and Boyd's driver's license photo were put on a new patrol flier and distributed to all patrol shifts and detectives as a BOLO. The information was emailed to all the outlying agencies with a warning that the subject may be portraying himself as an officer and is armed and dangerous."

"That's good," Brooks said. "We appreciate the help, nice work."

Cooper received a call on his private cell phone.

"Your house has to be demolished," the contractor said. "We've shored up the house enough for you to get in and remove your stuff."

"How long do I have?" Cooper asked.

"If we don't get started in two days, we will have to wait a month to get back to you," the contractor said.

"I'll get everything out in the next two days," Cooper said. "But why does it have to be demolished."

"The inspector reported that the house shifted on the foundation and several of the structure supporting walls were damaged or knocked down," the contractor said. "I could rebuild the house, but it would cost three times the amount of demolition and reconstruction. The insurance adjuster said they would not pay the higher costs. Unless you want to pay what insurance won't, we have to tear the house down and rebuild."

"Okay, rebuild it is," Cooper said.

Cooper spoke to the team.

"I won't be available for the next two days while I empty my house," Cooper said.

They understood and said they would keep him informed on the case if anything changed.

He regarded Jennifer and jokingly said, "See you at home, Honey."

Everyone laughed and Jennifer rolled her eyes as she waved goodbye.

They began to view the list of names and discovered 31 names left on the list with birthdays in the months of October, November, and December. This was still too many names to put surveillance on each possible victim, but they were getting close and needed one more break.

"Angie, why don't you call the chief and find out if he will let us use some volunteers," Brooks said. "He and I aren't on the best terms right now so it may be easier for you to get him to agree."

"Sure, but why?" asked Angie.

"We can use some of the volunteers to call possible victims and give them a heads up," Brooks said.

"That's a fantastic idea," Angie said. "They can give the women a brief on what to look for."

The chief agreed to allow volunteers to make the calls. As Angie left he asked her to send Jennifer to the office.

Jennifer was greeted at the chief's officer door.

"The captain will be joining us," the chief said.

The captain arrived in the chief's office within minutes.

"I will be attending a city council meeting in a few weeks to explain why they should retain me as chief," he said. "My position is appointed and is only for a year at a time. If the city council is not happy with the direction of the police department, they might fire me and find someone else to take over."

Okay, but what does that have to do with me?" Jennifer said puzzled.

"I want to be able to tell the council that the serial killer has been caught. I also want to say that many of the old timers are retiring and the department will be bringing in new and younger recruits with more energy and drive. I want to start by getting rid of Brooks. He's a leader and example among the old timers, and if he goes, many others will too."

"Why are you telling me this?" Jennifer asked.

"I'm getting to that," the chief curtly said. "I want you to keep an eye on Brooks for me and make note of any mistakes or policy violations that he commits. If you get a serious enough violation I can get rid of him. I will find a way to get rid of him and you'll be on the fast track to any position you want, or you'll be on the way out with Brooks. Brooks thinks he's untouchable and fights the administration at every turn. I need to have an ally on my side to get things done the way I want without the old timers resisting my efforts."

"Can I think about it?" Jennifer asked.

"Keep this conversation between the three of us or you may find yourself in the same sinking ship as Brooks," the chief said.

Jennifer exited the chief's office. When she was out of sight, she reached in her jacket pocket and turned off the recorder. She rejoined the team and didn't say a word about the meeting.

The team began to check for any paper trail that Boyd left. They examined credit card receipts, bank transactions, legal documents, contracts filed and even did address and information searches through the web sites that claim to be able to find anyone. They found nothing new.

CHAPTER 24

Brooks received a call from his daughter.

"We'll be in town in three days. Can you pick us up at the airport?" Lexi asked.

"Of course I can," Brooks said.

This was going to work out right on time. Angie's condominium was going to be finished tomorrow and she would be gone in time for him to clean up and get ready for Lexi and Janet. He was excited now and forgot about the case for a few minutes. His excitement was short lived when the phone rang and he was informed that another murder had been found.

"The scene is another apartment with no signs of forced entry," the dispatcher said. "But your team should go and see what was found this time."

They headed to the car and he told the two women what he knew on the way. Jennifer was quiet and didn't talk, but Brooks kept glancing at her out of the corner of his eye. She eyed him as if she had grim news.

They arrived at the scene. They were asked to put on gloves and booties before doing the walk through with CSPT.

"We've already taken general photos and were going to start collecting evidence, but wanted you to see things before they were moved," the CSPT leader said.

When they entered, they again walked on the edges of the walkways so no possible evidence would be disturbed. They entered the bedroom where the murder occurred and they were all stunned.

"That dirty bastard," Brooks said.

Lying on the bed face down was a young woman stabbed to death with the letter C cut in her back. Next to her was a second young woman stabbed to death with an O cut in her back. The team was shocked and as the killer promised, surprised. They exited the apartment to gather themselves and talk to the man who found them.

Abby and Sherri were getting ready for lunch that afternoon. They made a salad and some pork steaks and were setting the table. Someone knocked on the door and Abby answered. She let the man in.

"Who is it?" Sherry asked.

She turned to look and momentarily stopped breathing. The man stood next to Abby with a knife to her throat.

"Don't make a sound or you're both dead," he said. "Now be a nice girl and come over here and tie your friend's hands, and do it tight."

"I'll do whatever you want, please don't hurt us," Sherri said. "Wait I've met you somewhere before."

She tied Abby's hands and her hands were tied behind her back.

"Let's walk to the bedroom and have a talk ladies," Boyd said.

Abby and Sherri sat with their backs facing Boyd. He began to remove Abby's clothes and she resisted. He pushed the knife up by Abby's neck and they both became motionless. He removed their pants.

"Now if you cooperate and keep quiet, everything will be fine," Boyd said.

Abby and Sherri agreed to do what he said. Abby glanced at Sherri and saw the fear in her face. This intensified Abby's fear. She knew Sherri wasn't afraid of anything. If Sherri showed this much fear, Abby realized they weren't going to live. With this horrifying knowledge, she lost her will to fight and gave up.

He put a pillow on Sherri's face while he assaulted Abby. When he was done assaulting Abby, he bit her several times. He copied his act with Sherri except he slapped her several times in the face and buttocks.

Boyd turned them both face down and wasted no time using his expert cutlery skills. He stared at the blood beginning to mix as the pools ran into each other.

"It's time to go," he thought to himself as he quickly left.

**

Brooks approached the shocked and grieving witness.

"What's your name son?" Brooks asked.

"I'm Ryan Jochim," he said.

"How do you know the victims?" Brooks asked.

"My girlfriend is the girl on the left of the bed. Her name is Abby Perry and the girl next to her is her roommate, Sherry Rickman."

"I am sorry for you loss," Brooks said. "Do you think you can answer some questions for me?"

"I'll do my best," Ryan said.

"Please, tell me what you know about these two young ladies," Brooks said.

"Okay," Ryan said. "Abby is 21, born October 26 and Sherry is 22 and born in July. Both girls worked at Victoria's Secret as clothing fitters and sales clerks. They've worked together since high school. I've been dating Abby for about six months, and Sherry's like a sister to me now."

Ryan stopped and composed himself. His voice had a deep tone of grief and sadness but he continued. With tears in his eyes and a catch in his throat, Ryan talked about Abby first.

"Abby grew up in a loving family that lived locally and they had a close relationship. Her parents were loving and caring and even welcomed me in as if I belonged in the family. They are a Christian family and often meet Abby and me at church on Sunday. We eat dinner with her family at least once a week and her mother is always asking if we have plans for the future. Her father is a little more reserved and somewhat intimidating since he's a retired cop. He doesn't say much, but when he does, it is funny."

"Abby, Sherry and I were together last night until midnight," Ryan said. "At midnight I dropped them off and went home to get some sleep before work today."

"What time did you go to work?" Brooks asked.

"At 8 am, and worked until almost one. I went to Abby's for a late lunch around 1 p.m.."

"What happened when you arrived here?" asked Brooks.

"I found the girls and immediately left the apartment and called police," Ryan said. "I didn't touch anything other than the front door knob, which was unlocked when I got here. That's not uncommon though, because the girls often have friends in and out all the time. "

"Did you know Sherry's a year older than Abby and helped her get the job," Ryan said. "She and Abby worked the same schedule for about a year and were like two peas in a pod. They never fought and often shared each-others clothes. Sherry would come to dinner with Abby's family occasionally, since her family lived in Florida."

"Sherry graduated high school in Florida and moved to Seattle right after graduation. She had a rough childhood in Florida and wanted to get away from some of the histrionics and bullies that plagued her for years. She never returned home, but loved her parents very much. They called Sherry at least once a week and talked for hours at a time. Sherry was shy, and Abby was more outspoken. Together they attracted attention wherever they went. They were both beautiful. With Abby's bubbly personality and Sherry's wit, once she opened up, they were the life of the party."

"Can you think of anyone who would want to hurt the girls?" Angie asked.

He thought for a minute and obviously remembered something.

"We met a guy when we were in a bar playing darts the other night," Ryan said. "We needed a fourth person to play team darts and a guy asked to play on our team. We let him play with us and as the night wore on, he was getting pushy for Sherry to go out with him. By the time the game was over that night, she didn't want to see him again and seemed creeped out by him. She said he reminded her of a stalker who doesn't grasp when to quit. She was pretty drunk, but sober enough to want to stay away from him."

"Do you remember his name?" Brooks asked. "What did he look like?"

"He's an average guy and I think his name is Bradford something," Ryan said. "But I'm not sure. He's in his mid-thirties, or so, and kept trying to get Sherry to give him her phone number. She made it clear that she didn't date older men and he would not stop. After the game was over, we sat down away from him. He kept staring at us through the bar, so we left around midnight. Other than that, everyone loved Sherry and Abby."

"Do you know where Bradford lives?" Brooks asked.

"I don't know exactly, but Bradford asked us if we wanted to party at his place that was nearby," Ryan said. "We told him no and he kept insinuating that we'd have more fun in private. That's about the time we finished playing darts and separated from him. He was still at the bar when we left."

"What's the name of the bar you were at?" Angie asked.

"It's a college bar called The New Age Dungeon," Ryan said.

"Please call if you think of anything else that might help," Angie said.

Ryan was returned to his vehicle.

Brooks called the reserve office and asked the reserves to contact apartments around the bar Ryan had given them.

"Ask your reserves to contact apartment managers and ask if they have a tenant named Bradford or Clayton Boyd," Brooks said.

Angie contacted the patrol unit supervisor and asked the patrols to search for the stolen car in the same area.

Jennifer was in autopsy with the two bodies. Angie and Brooks joined her. She already completed the initial parts of the exam of Abby, while a coworker was completing Sherry's exam. Angie witnessed Abby's examination, while Brooks followed Sherry's autopsy. Brooks felt as if he upset Jennifer somehow, since she had been acting distant and odd.

Jennifer noted that Abby had been subjected to the same sexual assault as the others. She had her hands and feet tied after the assault. She had been stabbed, and a subsequent cut wound administered while she was face down. The wound shaped the letter C in her back. She had six bite marks on her chest and stomach. One below each breast, one above her navel, one below her navel, and one on each side of the last one.

Sherry's autopsy was the same as Abby's down to the bite marks except that Sherry's wound was deeper and applied with more force. The handle of the knife bruised her skin from being forcefully pushed against her when the blade penetrated its full length. She also had bruising on her cheek as if someone slapped her hard. Sherry's buttocks had been repeatedly slapped before her death, leaving bruising as well. The killer appeared to be angry, or have something personal against Sherry. These marks would support what Ryan said, if the killer had been the one in the bar that night.

Neither woman had any trace of the killer on her. Was it Boyd? How had Boyd controlled them both at the same time? Did he kill one and wait for the other? Had he threatened to kill one to control the other? Only Boyd knew these answers and Brooks intended to get them.

The CSPT report would not shed much new light on the serial killer either. They had not found any fingerprints, DNA or fibers not attributed to the girls. The only thing new was the note. It read, "You got too close early on, I had to make some plans. I sabotaged a sewer line, to distract your friends, and you step in and let her stay, and changed my plans again. I had to crash a house you know, to divide your team some more. Now I need to take a shot, to divide your team for sure. I had time to kill these two, and send them on to heaven. I hope you like my little surprise, I'm on to number eleven."

Cooper called in for an update after listening to the news. They told him about the note and that no new evidence had been found.

"We're pretty sure Boyd is the killer so we have to find him before the next victim," Brooks said.

"I'll be done moving things in the morning so I'll be back to help," Cooper said. "Have you reviewed the letters to see what they spelled?"

"No, but that's a good idea," Brooks said.

The team sat down and went through the letters. They wrote them down to check if it spelled anything. The letters thus far were, LANOEEYLBYDCO. They could not make sense of these letters yet.

CHAPTER 25

As they were talking, Brooks received a call from the chief.

"Gather your team and come to the captain's office for a briefing," the chief said.

Brooks called Cooper's phone and said, "Listen."

He put his phone in his pocket and headed for the meeting.

"We can't spare any more people for a new special assignment," the captain said.

"What does that mean?" asked Angie.

"During a recent transport from the court to the jail, the driver sustained a gunshot wound and the bus crashed. Three inmates were killed and two escaped."

"What's this have to do with us?" asked Brooks.

"One inmate was found within a mile of the bus because he was too injured to continue running," the captain continued, ignoring Brooks. "He's been taken to the hospital for treatment and will remain under guard until he can be returned to jail. The missing inmate that escaped is none other than Marvin Deltin."

"You've got to be kidding me," Brooks said.

"They tracked him for two miles using the tracking dogs," the captain said. "They found his orange jumpsuit at a convenience store dumpster. A department store reported being robbed and having men's clothing stolen by a man in an orange suit. Deltin's trail ended at the state ferry dock.

"Three ferries left the dock between the time Deltin escaped and when the dogs ended their tracking," the chief said. "One boat left too early for Deltin to be able to get on it. The other two went to Bremerton and Vashon Island. Both agencies were notified of the escape and that Deltin's possibly in the area. The local news media has been alerted and is doing live broadcasts with information on Deltin, and a number to call if he's seen."

"I'm pulling Angie and Cooper off the task force until Deltin's captured," the captain said. "You're strictly to work on coordinating and updating new information on Deltin coming in through the hotline. Angie, you're on your own until Cooper returns to assist you. You'll forward any information received to the agency Public Information Officer so he can disseminate leads to the media."

Brooks and Jennifer, you'll be working the case on your own," the captain continued. "You may only have a couple of days to resolve the case before the killer's gone. Christmas is around the corner and he said he would be done, so you had better get to work.

He excused everyone but Jennifer.

"Have you thought about the conversation the other day?" the chief asked.

"I have," Jennifer said. "I've been scrutinizing Brooks since. I haven't seen anything yet, but will keep track of him as much as I can."

"You can go places if you get enough on Brooks for the chief to force him to retire," the captain said as the chief nodded.

She left the office not feeling good about herself, but she didn't want to be on the chief's list of people to get rid of either. She waited until she was out of sight and checked the recorder.

When Jennifer returned to Brooks, she found him in lather, ready to rip someone's head off.

"The chief and captain are making it impossible to catch the killer when he's reassigning the team to menial crap," Brooks said. "I can't believe they would make such an ignorant decision that was so detrimental to a case of this magnitude. I can't wait for those two to find something else to do and retire. I hope I'm still around when they leave so I can give them an appropriate one-finger salute. This is what happens when you promote the ass kisser rather than the guy with the most knowledge of the job."

He continued on a rampage for about ten minutes before she returned. He apologized for the outburst.

"We need to refocus and get back on track for tomorrow," Brooks said.

In the morning, they began to brainstorm what other avenues they should examine to find the whereabouts of Boyd.

"If we have nothing to follow up on in the serial killer case we can work the Deltin case," Brooks said.

This would allow the team to get back together and get this case solved. After reviewing evidence and videos all day, they had nothing new and headed out to meet the rest of the team. The four members met at The Padded Cell for a couple of drinks. They vented about the ridiculous decision to separate the team when they were making headway, but were not surprised.

Cooper began to tell a story of when the chief and captain were on patrol together.

"They were in a foot pursuit of a burglary suspect," Cooper said. "This particular pursuit was caught on the chief and captain's body cameras. The video shows the chief on the heels of the suspect with the captain shortly behind them both. The video shows the chief tripping on the only item in the alley within twenty feet of him, a crack in the road. He tumbled down the alley as the captain passes him. The captain almost reaches the suspect, slips on some wet paper, does a tuck and roll, and gets back on his feet."

"Are you making this up?" asked Angie.

"It's true," Cooper said.

"Go on," Angie said.

"By then the chief is in front of the captain and has a huge hole in the seat of his pants. The captain's laughing on the video while still running. They both begin to close the gap on the suspect when the chief dives and misses him. The captain trips over the chief when he tries to jump over him. The captain tore a muscle in his leg and limps off. This ended the pursuit and the suspect got away."

They all laughed and commented on the quality of their fearless leaders.

Cooper told Brooks "Tell the story about the pond on the mountain property."

"No," Brooks replied.

The girls persisted.

"Okay," Brooks said. "When I was a rookie I responded to a warrant service. I and two other officers from the county were dispatched to serve multiple felony warrants on a subject that lived on the side of a mountain towards Tiger Summit, near Auburn. It snowed and was still icy towards the top. When we arrived, the three of us parked out of sight of the house and slowly walked up. As we approached, we spotted several manmade ponds on the side of the hills, one with a fence around it. We later found out that the suspect had already seen us. When we approached the three-story house, we heard music coming from a nearby barn. We knocked on the door of the house with no response. We approached the barn with music playing and knocked on that door. We announced we were the police and had a warrant. The music turned down and we realized we had the right building. We knocked again and the music turned off with no one coming out."

"Two of the officers walked around the barn and secured all but the door that I was at. As the other two tied the door to the barn together with bailing twine, the suspect emerged. He was 6'3" and almost 280 pounds. When he started to exit, he had a foot long screwdriver in his hand. I pointed my gun at him and commanded him to drop the weapon. When he was almost ten feet away, he put down the screwdriver. The other two officers arrived and we formed a half moon around the suspect, about ten feet apart. He still would not comply with demands and kept saying to shoot him because he was going to lose the property anyway. He took off running between the other two officers and ran through two streams of pepper spray. All three of us began to pursue him, but it was winter and icy. As the first officer got ahold of the suspect's shirt, he slipped on the ice and lost the grip he had. The second officer attempted to trip him and lost his footing in the process, falling down as well. The suspect's feet were caught together by the trip and he fell, head butting his pickup on the way down."

"By now I was on him as he got up, until I slipped and fell," Brooks said. "The suspect and I both got up at the same time and the pursuit was on again. The other two officers were behind but coming up fast. I saw a frozen pond up ahead with a fence around it. The suspect began to lean to one side of the pond as if he was going to turn right at the pond. I was going to tackle him when he turned at the fence. It was going to be a violent collision, but nothing new. When he reached the pond, he didn't turn right. He dove head first through the ice and into the chilling pond. When he surfaced, he was screaming about how cold he was, but he continued to break ice while swimming to the other side of the pond. The three of us walked to the other side of the pond and waited. When the suspect arrived, he refused to get out of the water. He kept saying that if he got out, he would lose his property. He was also screaming about how cold he was, but his face and eyes were burning from the pepper spray. I told him that if he did not come out of the water he would be pepper sprayed again and it would not make things better."

The others were riveted by the story and Brooks continued.

"He finally came out of the water, shaking from cold with his face burning," Brooks said. "As I approached to handcuff him, he tried to punch me and was hit with a Taser. Unfortunately, this resulted in his nerves being overloaded and caused an immediate release of his bowels, filling his pants and making for an uncomfortable, hour-long ride to the jail. He spent the ride sitting in his own mess, whining about his face burning and suffering from hypothermia from the pond. I'm not a tyrant so I gave him two blankets and opened the back window far enough to cool his face. Instead of charging the suspect with resisting arrest and attempted assault, I cut him some slack and booked him on the felony warrants. I didn't feel it was necessary to pile on the guy, and karma had already gotten him enough that day."

"Now that's funny," Angie said. "You should write a book about your career.

"I'd probably get rich and retire," Brooks said with a laugh.

"You have to tell the beagle story Coop," Brooks said. "Before the team is broken up."

"I don't have time tonight, but I will before this case is over," Cooper said.

The team headed out with a feeling that the chief was trying to make them fail.

In the middle of the night, Cooper and Angie were called out because Deltin may have been found. They were both briefed.

"A homeowner heard a noise in his daughter's bedroom and thought a stranger was in the house," the dispatcher said. "He grabbed his gun and rushed down the hall. When he opened the door to his daughter's room, a man was standing over his daughter with a knife. The man was trying to get her out of bed and out the window. The father rushed the intruder and they began to wrestle when he pulled the trigger on his gun. The intruder kept fighting and the father fired two more shots."

CSPT was on the scene processing the daughter's room. The chief requested that Cooper and Angie interview family members. They were told the family was being transported to the office.

Cooper met the dad and found out his name was William Mercer.

155

William was asked to relay the events of the evening. He was still full of adrenaline. He was violently shaking, wide-eyed and still amped up.

"My daughter, Maddison, watched television with me until 9 p.m.," Mercer said. "My wife, Shannon, had gone to bed early because she works early in the morning. My daughter went to bed shortly after nine and I went to bed at 10 p.m. About an hour later, I heard a noise from my daughter's room that sounded like a man's voice. I grabbed my gun out of the nightstand and ran to my daughter's room. I saw the earlier news reports of an escaped pedophile in the area and was concerned. When I opened the door, a man stood over my daughter with a knife in his hand."

He stopped talking and Cooper prompted him by asking, "What happened next Mr. Mercer?"

"I entered the room and told the man to get away from my daughter," Mercer said. "We began to wrestle and I fired the gun once. The man continued to fight and I fired a couple more times to defend my family. I think I fired three times but after the first shot, I kept firing until the man was no longer threatening my daughter."

Angie interviewed Maddison. Her voice was quiet and trembling, she was crying, and her hands were shaking.

"Are you okay to tell me what happened tonight Maddie?" asked Angie.

"I was in bed sleeping," Maddie said. "I woke up when a man put his hand over my mouth. The man told me if I made a noise he would kill my family and me. He asked if I understood and I nodded my head. He took his hand away and said I was going to come out the window with him. I shook my head no and he showed me a knife. I nodded and began to get out of bed. As I got up, I heard my dad say something and the man started moving towards me. Before he got to me, my dad grabbed him and they were wrestling. As they wrestled, I heard a loud noise and the man fell to the floor. My dad rushed me out of the room, to my mom and they called the police."

Cooper interviewed Maddison's mother, Shannon.

"What happened tonight Mrs. Mercer?"

"I went to bed early," Mrs. Mercer said. "William woke me up. He told me he thought someone was in Maddie's room. He grabbed his gun and headed to Maddie's room. About fifteen-seconds later, I heard gunshots and rushed down the hall. My husband and daughter met me in the hallway. He told me to call the police because he shot someone. We stayed in the living room until the police arrived and drove us here. Can I see my daughter and husband? I don't know anymore and don't want to talk about it."

They were reunited.

Cooper and Angie went back to the scene to talk to CSPT and see if they had an ID yet. When they arrived, the body had been removed, and CSPT was fingerprinting the outside of the windowsill.

"We found several prints and put the prints into the computer," said the CSPT member. "We're still processing."

CSPT was in the residence for another hour before coming out with a small bag of evidence. After they packed up the processing truck and were taking a break, Angie approached.

"Did you get an ID on the intruder?" Angie asked.

"Let me check the computer," the CSPT member said. "Yes, we have a match. The fingerprints on the windowsill and inside the window belonged to Marvin Deltin."

Angie asked for a copy of the report after it was completed and they agreed to send the report to the task force office.

Cooper and Angie headed home feeling sure that Deltin would not be making it to prison after all. His days of kidnapping, torture and murder were probably over for good. Justice had been served and didn't take forty years or more. Neither one of them would lose any sleep over Deltin, but now they were back on the Letters of Death case if the autopsy confirmed their suspicion.

In the morning, Jennifer and Brooks were surprised to see the other two at the task force office.

"Deltin may not be a problem after a fatal shooting last night," Cooper said.

"Really, what happened?" asked Brooks.

They were briefed about last night's incident and that Deltin was probably dead. None of them were upset that he had been killed, but had mixed feelings about him not spending the rest of his life in prison waiting to become a victim himself and maybe realizing what his victims felt.

CHAPTER 26

The DNA from the first two cases finally returned from the FBI lab. The FBI found a match. This match was a little mysterious.

"We got the DNA reports back but it doesn't make sense," Angie said.

"Go ahead and read it so we all have the same info," Brooks said.

"The DNA returned to Bradford Wielke," Angie said. "This is where it gets weird. Wielke's been dead for ten years. He was allegedly killed in a plane crash at the age of 25. According to the FAA crash report attached here, Bradford's body had been found in the plane crash but was too badly destroyed for DNA analysis or dental comparison. He almost burned up completely.

"Maybe Wielke wasn't in the plane after all," Brooks said.

"The report goes on to say that the smudged fingerprints examined, were not smudges at all," Angie said. "They were fingerprints of someone who had been severely burned, as if the skin melted the fingerprints off. A few slight ridges of a print were present, but in viewing the smudges in comparison to known prints, the only ones that were somewhat similar were of criminals who attempted to melt their own fingerprints off leaving a smudgy melted skin type impression. Wielke has the same date of birth that Boyd gave at his girlfriend's murder scene. I also remembered Brooks telling us about Boyd's burn gloves on his hands. I understand these gloves come off, but are worn by severe burn victims. I'll investigate Wielke and requested a driver's license photo."

"Did you get it yet?" Cooper said excitedly.

"I received the photo in my email," Angie said. "The photo's a younger version of Clayton Boyd. Boyd/Wielke must have had his gloves off at the first two scenes in order to leave the smudged fingerprints. I think we know who the killer is and need to let everyone else know."

Cooper compiled a history on Wielke and emailed everyone a copy.

"I hate to leave now," Brooks said. "But I have to pick up Janet and

Lexi from the airport and won't be back today. I want to stay, but I won't let my daughter down right now. If you need me, I will be at home with my family, but won't be available until after 5 p.m.

"Okay Brooks, go enjoy your family for a while," Angie said.

"I don't want to be called unless you get a break in this case," Brooks said. "I don't care if it's confirmed that Deltin's been killed. If I'm needed I'll come back to work, but otherwise you're more than capable of handling the case."

Brooks met Lexi and Janet at the airport.

"I would have rented a truck if I knew how many suit cases you'd be bringing," Brooks said.

The ladies rolled their eyes at each other, hugged him, and got in the car. At his house, they unloaded all their bags and went out to the deck. As they began to get caught up on each other's lives, he felt a sense of peace and harmony that he had not felt since this case began. He was enjoying the moment and completely left the case at the office. Lexi told him about her career and that she met someone new.

"We've been dating for a few weeks, but nothing serious because we're both busy with our careers," Lexi said.

"I haven't been dating anyone and don't want to at this point in my life," Janet admitted. "I'm happy being Lexi's mom. I've been busy trying to get healthier by eating better and drinking less. I even found a gym that isn't full of a bunch of overstuffed guys who think they are God's gift to the world. I've lost almost 30 pounds and feel terrific."

"You look fantastic," Brooks said. "Maybe later I can feel how fantastic."

"You haven't changed," Janet said with a smile.

She didn't say no.

He and Janet had been intimate several times since they had been divorced. They could not live under the same roof as a couple, but truly still cared for each other.

"Do you want to sleep in the guest room with Lexi or in my bed," Brooks asked. "I can sleep on the couch."

"We're both adults and slept together for over ten years so I think we'll be fine for a little over a week. If you can behave, I can too."

"You can have this conversation without me," Lexi said. "And it's still gross to listen to you talk like that."

They laughed and started getting ready for bed.

The last thing Lexi said was, "Goodnight and keep your hands to yourselves."

CHAPTER 27

That same night, the chief was in the city council meeting when he was informed that they planned to do a nationwide search for a new chief.

"I'm confused," the chief said. "I thought you were happy with my work to this point."

"We don't want to get into reasons, but are requesting you start your retirement paperwork immediately," the counsel said.

"Why?" asked the chief.

The city council president pulled out an audiotape. As the tape played, the chief recognized it as the conversation he and the captain had with Jennifer. On the tape, he listened to his own voice threatening Brooks' career and the career of many other well-liked officers. Many of the officers he planned to target were known by the council and well liked by them.

"You and the captain are on paid suspension until your retirement paperwork is completed," said the counsel president. "If you contest the forced retirement, the audio tape will be released to the city attorney and the media."

"Okay, I'll retire and tell the captain as well," the chief said.

"You both have eight hours to clear out the office. An interim chief is being brought in while we recruit possible candidates for your jobs," the counsel president said.

The chief returned to his office and called the captain in. A few minutes later, the captain went to his own office and began to pack his things as well. The task force soon found out the chief and captain were retiring effective immediately, and that a new chief would be in the office by the end of the day.

"What brought this on I wonder?" asked Cooper.

"I don't know, but it sure is odd," said Angie.

"Well, maybe it's for the best," said Jennifer with a knowing smile.

They were all surprised and tried to figure out why the two had such a change in career paths. They were also concerned whether the new chief would come in and want to change the entire department to suit his goals. This happened several times in their careers and they were too old to want to put up with another complete shuffle.

The team received notification that patrol officers were in pursuit of the stolen vehicle the killer had been using. They were headed south on Pacific Highway currently going by the airport. Seattle Police were in pursuit and had been joined by the King County Sheriff's Office. They also notified the other agencies where the pursuit was headed.

"Let's jump in the car and parallel the pursuit," Cooper said. "You never know when they may need another hand."

"I'll drive," Angie said.

"No, I'll drive," Cooper said. "I get to drive in pursuits."

The team jumped in the car and headed down I-5 in the direction of the pursuit. They were not allowed to join the pursuit in an unmarked detective car, but wanted to be close if the killer was captured. The pursuit entered Federal Way at a speed of over 100 miles per hour. The officers were describing the weather conditions, the violations of the suspect, amount of traffic, road conditions, and speeds.

This allowed the officer's supervisor to judge whether the pursuit was too dangerous for the public. It also allowed a supervisor to judge the stress level of the officer leading the pursuit based on his voice on the radio. Officers start talking faster, or in a higher pitch, when they are overstressed during a pursuit. Evaluating these things has allowed many supervisors to terminate pursuits over minor offenses before an innocent person in the public is hurt or killed.

The pursuit was continuing into Tacoma and was headed towards the Tacoma Dome. Cooper was aware of a scheduled concert in an hour and feared the suspect would be lost in the traffic heading to the dome. Within ten minutes, the officers leading the pursuit called in and said the suspect caused an accident by the dome. The result was a collision blocking their path and the pursuit was over. They requested other units in the area search for the suspect. Unfortunately, the suspect was able to get away, for now. After searching the area, the task force headed back to their office disappointed.

Since Cooper had not been in the office the last few days he had not checked his email. In his email, he found an information file on Wielke/ Boyd. A detective he talked to completed it and emailed the report earlier.

"I received a personal history file on Wielke," Cooper said. "The file says Wielke lived with his parents early in life. His father had been an abusive alcoholic and beaten him and his mother regularly. He grew up watching his mother lie for his father anytime she was beaten, or if she had to go out while she still had visible bruises. When he was ten, his father left the family. He moved from his mother's home to foster homes the same year. By the age of 15, he had been arrested several times for animal cruelty. He progressed to domestic abuse of his girlfriends, shortly after that. Wielke was arrested for arson at age 17 and 19. During the same time, Wielke was arrested for sexual assault, but the charges were dropped. At age 20, he was convicted of rape and sentenced to five years of probation. At age 21, he was arrested for rape and felony assault."

"It sounds like a copy of the FBI profiler's report," Jennifer said.

"Go on," Angie said.

"He severely beat his girlfriend after she refused to let him tie her up. He bit her and whipped her with a riding crop," Cooper said. "She agreed to drop the charges if he attended mandatory counseling and paid for the counseling she required. He attended the counseling and stopped when he met enough of the requirements. Before he was allegedly killed in the plane crash he had been charged with rape and attempted murder. He forced a woman to have sex with him and beat her so severely she slipped into a coma. He left her for dead thinking she would not come out of the coma, but he was wrong. Two weeks later, she awoke and gave a detailed account of her rape and beating to the police. Wielke had been arrested and charged, but was able to post bond and be released. While awaiting trial his plane crashed and he had been presumed dead until his DNA showed up at the current crime scenes."

The team was amazed at how close the life story of Wielke had been compared to the FBI profilers report. The profiler had been right on the money. It was another long day and time to go home. They agreed to leave Brooks alone and let him catch up in the morning.

As the team left the office, they were told to be in the new chief's office at 9:30 am for a briefing on the case.

Before the morning meeting, they updated Brooks on how close they were and had him read Wielke's file. At 9:30 am they were outside the chief's office waiting to be brought in for the briefing. When they walked in, Cooper stopped and said, "Marshall, what are you doing here."

"I've been asked to fill in as the interim chief while the counsel interviewed for the position," Marshall said. "I expressed interest in this job two years ago, but never heard from anyone until last week. I jumped at the chance and am hoping to be the next permanent chief. I like Colorado but would enjoy working here."

The team spent the next three hours filling him in on crime scene photos, files from other states, the history of the suspect, and all the evidence that had been found so far.

"I won't allow you four to be involved in any other case until this is solved," Marshall said. "You are too close now. Keep me informed of any further developments. If an arrest is imminent, we should bring in the lead detectives from the other cases."

"That's an excellent idea chief," Brooks said. "If this is how you run your ship, I hope they keep you as chief after the interviews."

"Have you considered the letters as a word jumble," Marshall suggested. "Scramble the letters around and see if they spell something."

During the meeting, they received a call that another scene had been discovered like the last. The team began to leave.

"Can I ride along to see first-hand what type of situation you're dealing with?" the chief asked.

"You're the boss," Cooper said smiling.

They arrived and were met by CSPT. After putting on the booties and gloves, they walked into the scene. They found a woman face down with the letter T in her back and another woman to her right with the letter B.

"What kind of sick twisted dirt bag would do this to young women?" the chief asked.

The team nodded in agreement and left the scene, saying they would be waiting for the report.

Jennifer contacted her office and told them of the two women coming in. She said she would be in the office to process one and would like at least two others to assist with the procedures. The team sat down and put the letters together again. The letters now were, LANOEEYLYDCOTB.

The team rearranged the letters for almost an hour.

"I got it!" Angie exclaimed.

The team waited, and she used every letter. She wrote, CLAYTON LEE BOYD.

Jennifer had to leave for the exam of the first victim. This did not produce new evidence. The team was not surprised. When she completed the exam, she only found a couple of differences. These victims had been sexually assaulted like the others, but had been bitten seven times. Six of the bites were in the same position as the last victim but this time the bites below the navel were different. One was right below the navel as the other victims, and two were on the right side of the first one and one was on the left. When all seven bites were viewed together, they formed a morbid bite mark smiley face on the victim's stomach and chest.

The second victim's exam was the same as the first. Both victims had been sexually assaulted, tied up after the assault, and killed. Both victims had been stabbed through the heart while standing and the letter cut into them while face down. Both of these women had been bitten seven times, forming the bite mark smiley face on each of them.

The team did not have the identity of these two victims, since no ID's had been found this time. They assumed they were the two women on the lease, but wanted confirmation. Both had been fingerprinted and blood swabs taken from them for DNA if their prints weren't matched. Within an hour, they received a call with the fingerprint results. The first woman was identified as Brenda Jacobson and the second victim was Maggie Schuler.

Brenda and Maggie were doing their daily workout routine earlier that day. They planned to attend the yoga class at the gym in an hour. They were cleaning the kitchen when the doorbell rang. Brenda answered the door, while Maggie finished cleaning up. Brenda spoke to Officer Wielke and let him in.

He heard Maggie in the other room and quickly put the knife to Brenda's throat and told her to take him to the bedroom. He quickly tied her hands behind her back and put a gag in her mouth.

"Who is it?" Maggie asked with no reply. "Brenda?"

Wielke emerged from the bedroom and met Maggie in the kitchen.

"Oh hi," Maggie said. "Why are you here, officer?"

"I was talking to Brenda and she said you may be able to help," Wielke said. "She is back in the bedroom."

Maggie and Wielke walked to the bedroom. When Maggie opened the door she saw Brenda tied up and gagged on the bed. She turned to ask what was going on and he violently put her hands behind her back and shoved her to the bed. He tied her hands.

"If you two can cooperate, things will be much easier on you," Wielke said.

Maggie started to scream and was immediately gagged too.

Brenda had tears streaming down her face and an expression of sheer terror. Maggie was irate and waited for an opportunity to kill this man. Wielke sensed this and attacked Maggie first. He assaulted her as the others, and bit her numerous times. He tied her feet together and ended her life as he had all the others. He turned his focus to Brenda and mirrored the assault. He savored this attack and soaked in the traumatic expression on Brenda's face. After enjoying his work, he finally turned her over and stabbed the knife into her back. He watched as the life drained from her eyes and her blood pooled with Maggie's. He finished cutting his letters and departed. He only had one more scene to make and he would be gone.

***

Brooks found during the investigation into Brenda that little was revealed into her life. Brenda was a 23-year-old born in November. She was a grocery store clerk and lived in her apartment for two years. She had never been arrested but was listed as a victim of domestic violence when she was 18. Her fingerprints were in the system because her parents had her fingerprinted during a tour of the police station when she was in junior high.

Brenda was active in the community, working as a volunteer at the homeless shelter for women. She donated a large portion of her income to the shelter and only kept enough to get by. She believed in paying it forward. She originally grew up in Wyoming, but moved to Washington to pursue her passion of helping women in need. She had been close to her family and they had been notified of her death. Brenda had been roommates with Maggie for 18 months.

The investigation into Maggie's life was a little less rosy. She had been in an abusive relationship. That is how they met. She was living in the shelter. They made an instant friendship and Brenda found Maggie a job.

Maggie was hired cleaning houses for friends of Brenda's, and had done well since her divorce. Maggie came from a dysfunctional family and had been physically abused by her father. Her mother tried to protect her and loved her, but when her father was drunk, he was out of control. Maggie often stayed with friends when her father was drinking. She met a man like her father and fell into a repeat cycle. Eventually she left her husband to be on her own, but had trouble finding a job and ended up at the shelter. Maggie began to volunteer at the shelter and give back what she had been given.

Both women had clear criminal records. Maggie had two tickets for not wearing a seat belt. Other than that, everything discovered about these women led the team to believe that they probably had not provoked the killer to choose them. They were unlucky enough to be on the list that Zumwalt gave Wielke.

The CSPT report was almost a repeat of many others. The blood from the victims was found in the bedroom. They had somehow been controlled until they were tied up and killed. Again, a taunting note had been found with the women. This time it read, "Now I'm on to number 12 and then I'm gone for good. This time, save the ones you love, I mean it, you should. It's been fun and quite a rush with you upon my trail. If you don't catch me in two days, I know you never will. Goodbye my foe, you are quite good, but I think I will stay free. I feel quite certain by now, that you can't catch me."

CHAPTER 28

They had no more than two days to find Wielke or he would be gone for good. They updated the patrol fliers and made sure every car had several copies for the officers. They emailed more to the local agencies requesting assistance in locating the car and Wielke. Brooks was heading home to spend time with his family and the other three headed for a drink. They had four days before Christmas, but the killer had never gone more than two days without killing. They hoped the patrol units would find the car or Wielke before then.

The next afternoon Brooks was at work waiting for the team to return from lunch when Janet called to thank him.

"What are you talking about?" asked Brooks.

"You know," Janet said. "You sent an officer to get Lexi for her surprise. He said you planned a private tour of the stadiums, and arranged to meet the Seahawks. He said I was welcome to go, but I already made other plans."

"Janet, I didn't do that," Brooks said. "What was the officer's name?"

"I think he said Officer Wielke."

"I didn't send anyone to pick either of you up," Brooks said. "I didn't set up a private tour either. Stay calm. The serial killer we're searching for is named Wielke and he may have Lexi."

Janet began to panic.

"You know I won't let anything happen to her," Brooks said calmly. "Stay home in case she comes back or calls the house."

"Okay, but promise me she'll be fine."

"I'll make sure she's fine," Brooks said.

"I believe you," Janet said.

Brooks informed Cooper and Jennifer what happened and they were mortified. They stared at him with pity that made him sick to his stomach. He was furious now and wanted to kill Wielke rather than arrest him.

"I tried to contact Angie but her phone went straight to voicemail,"

Jennifer said. "I called her house and an officer answered. I asked why he was at Angie's house. The officer said that a neighbor called saying a woman was screaming inside and sounded like things were being broken in the condominium. The neighbor said he witnessed a man forcing Angie into a car before speeding off. He identified the car as a green Ford Escort."

The team comprehended what this meant. They lost a team member to Wielke and Brooks lost a daughter too. He hoped to find them before they were lost forever.

"An officer was here to take my statement," Janet said when Brooks answered his phone. "He told me to remain home in case anyone called and to lock the doors. I already locked everything. Have you heard anything new?"

"Not yet," Brooks said. "But we're working on it."

The team contacted the chief's office and told Marshall what happened. He made an emergency broadcast to the patrol units and told dispatch to hold all non-emergency calls. He requested every agency within 30 miles be notified of the situation.

Marshall contacted the news media and held a press conference in front of ten stations within fifteen minutes.

"Marvin Deltin is dead," Marshall said. "It's been confirmed, but we have a more pressing issue."

He gave a description of Wielke, his car, the two current hostages, and the last location Wielke had been seen in his vehicle. The press conference was broadcast over the TV and radio. Within ten minutes, they received 50 calls from citizens who had seen a car matching the description of Wielke's. Patrol units were scrambling to respond to as many calls as possible.

The King County Sheriff provided units to aid in the search. Brooks was reading over the calls that came in and one stood out. The caller said that he saw the suspect vehicle near an address on Ocean Drive. This address was within a few blocks of Brooks' house.

"A vehicle matching the description was seen near my house," Brooks said. "I'm gonna check on Janet. Stay alert and let me know if anything comes up."

"Go take care of Janet," Cooper said. "We got it from here."

He drove home and stopped a block away to view the house and check if anything appeared off. He walked up to his house from the blind side and everything looked normal. He drew his gun. He approached the front door and listened. He tried the handle and the door was locked. He felt his heart beating in his forehead. He inserted the key, unlocked the door, turned the handle and opened the door slightly. He listened again for anything out of place. Since he heard nothing, he entered slowly, standing inside the front door, and scanning the area. He found nothing in the living room or kitchen and no one was on the deck. He entered the hallway and heard a female voice in his bedroom. He cleared the house room by room until he reached the first bedroom door.

With his gun drawn, he opened the spare room door and found Angie face down all tied up on the bed. He entered quickly. No one else was in the room. He cautiously approached Angie on the bed. She had been stabbed through the heart from behind and an exclamation point cut into her back. She was dead.

He approached the bathroom and cleared it quickly. He moved toward the last room, his bedroom. He stood outside the door listening. He heard a male voice inside the door.

"Come on in and join the party," the voice said.

He briefly reached into his pocket, look at it, and put the object back. He took a deep breath and reached for the handle. He opened the door and Lexi and Janet were on the bed.

Janet was lying down and Lexi was sitting up. Both women had their hands tied behind their backs. Janet's feet were also tied. Wielke was sitting behind Lexi with a knife at her throat.

"Drop the knife Wielke," Brooks commanded.

"No, you drop your gun," Wielke said.

Brooks didn't move a muscle.

"I didn't expect you home so soon," Wielke said. "I have so much more fun planned and now it's ruined. I planned a little private time with each of the ladies before I disappeared again. Too bad I didn't get a chance to play with Angie before I killed her. She's quite a scrapper."

Brooks felt a sense of rage welling up inside him. He had to calm that feeling to stay sharp and focused.

"I Know everything you've done," Brooks said. "New York, Tennessee, Colorado, and now Seattle."

Wielke thought for a moment and began to talk.

"I remember the first woman I killed in New York. I never killed anyone before and was nervous and afraid. Killing someone each year was enough to keep my appetite in check."

"Why don't you and I step out and talk like men," Brooks said.

"After killing 12 women in New York I wanted somewhere new to hunt," Wielke said ignoring him. "I moved to Tennessee and killed every three weeks for almost a year. I got fussier about who I killed. I liked the challenge of killing women who put up a fight. I enjoyed the struggle as they fought for their lives. I bet you didn't know I killed one woman between New York and Tennessee. It was the first week of 2013. I can't remember where I was exactly. I had been driving for so long."

"Why don't you move the knife away from her neck and we can talk," Brooks said.

"Are you listening to me?" Wielke said angrily.

"Yes, I'm listening, but I can focus better if you move the knife away from her throat," Brooks said.

Wielke moved the knife off Lexi's throat, but kept the blade close to her.

"I killed 8 women in Tennessee before I got bored," he admitted.

This made Wielke laugh and Brooks recalled the message left in Tennessee.

Wielke glazed over as if he was in dreamland while he reminisced.

"I killed another woman between Tennessee and Colorado in September of 2013. I don't remember where because I was on the road. I enjoyed Colorado and perfected my killing skill. I only killed young athletic women in Colorado. The lead detective was on his way out the door and never got close to catching me."

Brooks let him keep talking. Wielke bragged about coming to Seattle and had not intended on ending his killing spree here.

"I heard of you when I lived in Colorado," Wielke said. "It was that case you did that attracted national media attention. I thought you would be a challenge for me and that's why I came."

"You came here for me?" Brooks asked. "Let her go and you can have me."

"I didn't think you'd get this close," Wielke said. "I've never had anyone get this close and I'm impressed. You realize, I have the upper hand and will be walking out of here.

Brooks said nothing.

"I know you're wondering how I met Zumwalt. We met in a bar one night when I first came to town. Zumwalt was singing the blues about not being able to keep a girlfriend. We started a conversation and I realized I could manipulate him and his police connection to find what I was searching for."

"Let the ladies go and you and I can stay here and talk as long as you want," Brooks said.

"I want you to know this," Wielke said. "I groomed Zumwalt for weeks and had him convinced he could keep a woman if he let me teach him. I moved in with Zumwalt and found even more resources to protect my trade. I used his ID and Tyvek suits to enter without resistance and leave without a trace."

"Why did you fake your death," Brooks asked.

Wielke smiled and asked, "Who investigates a dead man? I had to lay low for a few years while reinventing myself. I struggled to stay off the radar for that long. I figured I'd easily hide in a huge city like New York."

"Anything else you want me to know," Brooks asked.

"I also killed my mother," Wielke said. "But no one cared. As you have seen, I'll do anything to stay out of prison."

"I understood but can't let you leave with Lexi," Brooks said confidently. "Give up now."

Wielke stood up with Lexi.

"Time to leave," Wielke said.

Brooks understood it would be better to get Wielke out of this room so he only had one woman to worry about saving. He allowed Wielke to work his way towards the door and into the hallway.

Wielke was slowly backing down the hallway with Brooks following closely. He did not want to shoot and hit Lexi so he was relaxing his gun hand. When the time was right, he wouldn't suffer from muscle fatigue. They continued to exchange comments as Wielke worked his way to the front door.

"You're not leaving this house with Lexi," Brooks said.

Wielke disagreed. When they approached the front door, Lexi gave Brooks the signal he taught her and he got ready to strike. He steadied his shooting hand and prepared for the right moment. Lexi dropped her weight and pulled out of Wielke's grasp.

Brooks fired his weapon and hit Wielke in the left side of his face. He had not hit Wielke solidly because Lexi's head was in the way. Wielke was hit on the edge of his cheek leaving a horizontal bullet gouge down the left side of his face and taking half his ear off. Wielke reached for his face screaming, releasing Lexi in the process. She fell to the floor as Wielke ran out the front door. Brooks rushed to his daughter to comfort her and she grabbed him with the force of a grizzly bear. She was crying and shaking and did not want to let him go. He began to sob tears of joy that she was safe. As they calmed down, he felt a sense of hatred towards Wielke that he never felt before. He wanted this man dead.

After collecting himself and calming his daughter, he pulled the cell phone from his pocket.

"Cooper did they get him?"

"We heard the whole thing," Cooper said. "We were waiting outside for him when he ran out. You stalled him long enough for us to get set up. We recorded the conversation and the prosecutor will love every word."

"Thanks for the cell phone idea," Brooks said. "Can you send the medics to check on my family?"

Janet and Lexi were untied.

"Are you okay?" Brooks asked them.

"We're fine, a little scared still," they responded.

Janet jumped up after being untied and hugged Brooks, calling him a crazy bastard. He smiled and hugged her back. He kissed her on the head.

"I promised you I wouldn't let anything happen," Brooks said.

"I know you would die before you let anything happen to us," Janet said. She kissed him passionately and said. "I've always known that."

Lexi ran over and hugged them both. With a sudden realization she asked," where's Angie?"

"She didn't make it dear," Brooks said. "I'm sorry."

They felt tremendous sadness and guilt that they survived and Angie had not.

After everyone had time to settle down, they were asked to speak to a detective to give their statements. Everyone was eventually interviewed and released. Brooks and his family all sat on the deck to forget the events of the day. They began to come down off their adrenaline rush and they became exhausted. They headed to bed and before she fell asleep, Lexi heard her parents messing around. The last thing she thought before she fell asleep was, "Yuck!"

In the office, the new chief came in and asked permission to interrupt.

"I notified the other agencies and the lead detectives from each case will be here to interview Wielke," Marshall said. "Wielke's being evaluated over night for a head injury. He'll be treated for his injuries and held in a secure hospital room until tomorrow. He's agreed to be interviewed, but only by Brooks and Cooper. If you have your interview questions ready, I'm giving the task force the day off with pay. After this case, I wish I had the authority to give you at least a week off with pay when the interviews are completed."

The team retired to Brooks' deck to celebrate with Lexi and Janet. Cooper and Jennifer were being affectionate with each other all night. They didn't talk about the case but sat telling stories of old from different stages of their careers. Cooper finally told the beagle story.

"I was a young patrol officer. I was working patrol when a vehicle left a known drug house. The vehicle had several lights burned out and the driver was not wearing a seatbelt. I initiated a traffic stop and the driver turned into a gas station. I pulled in behind the driver as a motorhome drove in from the other way and stopped at the gas pump next to us. I exited my car to approach the driver. The motorhome owner had gotten out and let his beagle out of the side. I approached the driver and smelled burnt marijuana emanating from the car. As I was talking to the driver, the beagle walked around his car sniffing and stopping. The dog stopped next to me, barked at the driver, and sauntered back to the motorhome. I smelled marijuana in the car and asked the driver if he carried drugs inside. Having seen the dog the driver said, "Your drug dog already smelled my stash so I may as well give it to you." The driver handed a bag of marijuana and a small baggy of meth to me. I stood dumbfounded and laughing to myself. I ended up arresting the driver on a felony drug charge because some random beagle walked by my traffic stop."

Everyone laughed and called it a night. They wanted to be fresh for what might be a long couple of days interviewing Wielke.

As the profiler predicted, Wielke was more than willing to brag for days about his murderous exploits, from New York to Seattle. The case was closed, the killer captured and the team all assigned back to their regular assignments.

During a morning press conference, Marshall announced the capture of the serial killer, and that he had been chosen as the new chief.

"This conference will be brief because I have more pressing duties to take care of," Marshall said.

He came into the task force office.

"I'm recommending the task force for a commendation medal for the work you did to solve this case," Marshall said. "I'm recommending that Brooks and Cooper be moved to the homicide investigation squad. Angie will be getting her name added to the Law Enforcement Officer's Memorial in Burien at the Police Training Center. Angie will also receive a full law enforcement burial service. I want to speak to you, Jennifer, in private to find out your career goals."

"Thanks for taking care of Angie," Brooks said.

"I have more news," Marshall said. "After two days of testimony by witnesses, the six-person panel of jurors and the judge in the coroner's inquest cleared you in the Jonathon Malcom shooting. The jurors only took thirty minutes to decide the proper outcome of the case and the judge concurred. The case is closed and you can put the shooting behind you. I understand that's easier said than done, and if you ever need counseling or support, let me know."

The two officers would deal with the effects of taking a human life forever.

Several days later Angie received her burial service. Three thousand law enforcement officers attended. The weather was a cold and drizzly. When the service began, a ray of sunshine broke through the clouds and shown on Angie's casket. The bagpipes were playing. Glancing around the service hundreds of known tough guys were standing with tears streaming down their faces. This included Brooks and Cooper. After the service concluded, Angie received a 21-gun salute. Marshall presented the folded flag from her coffin to her mother and concluded the ceremony.

Before the team left, Marshall asked them to meet him in his office.

When they arrived, Marshall set up four chairs opposite to his. He also had five shot glasses and a bottle of 30-year-old scotch, courtesy of Cooper.

"Please sit," Marshall said.

He poured five shots of scotch, handed each one a glass, placing the remaining shot glass on Angie's vacant chair.

"She may be gone but she is here with us in spirit," Marshall said. Each member of the team made a toast to Angie and drank the shot together. When they glanced at Angie's chair, her shot glass was empty too.

ABOUT THE AUTHOR

B. D. Harris

B.D. Harris is a retired Police Officer. He also spent more than a decade working in both men's and woman's prisons. He spent over 20 years in his law enforcement career, and his encounters have allowed him to see into the mind of criminals. He has created his fictional characters based off his own experiences.

B.D. is the father of four wonderful children. He has been married to the love of his life for almost two decades. He grew up in Montana and moved to Washington as a teenager. He has lived his entire life in Montana and Washington State.

Made in the USA
Middletown, DE
29 June 2019